JOYCE
CAROL
OATES

THE
TRIUMPH
OF
THE
SPIDER
MONKEY

Santa Barbara
Black Sparrow Press
1976

slowly we are overrunning the earth
spidermonkeys twittering climbing leaping leering
on broken banjos

the Jukebox of the 40's could not cage us in
stunned, the arm of the mechanism pauses
paralyzed

when the Spider Monkeys inside
open soul-doors to us spidermonkeys skinned alive
the magic of My Passage on Earth
will be just another headline

THE TRIUMPH
OF THE
SPIDER MONKEY

1

Nativity

Noise, vibrations, murmuring nosey crowd of bastards with nothing else to do but gawk—grunting sweating bastard in a uniform reaching in and grabbing me out of the darkness and delivering me to light—

—to lights, that is—

Holding me up to those lights. *A baby! A baby still alive!*

Time: 6:05 PM. Date: February 14, 1944.

Delivered by the Master Key endowed by its creator to open all the lockers, foot-lockers renting for 25c for 24 hours—delivered by some amazed outraged bastard in a uniform to the surprise and anger and gradual disappointment of the crowd (*It's still alive . . . a baby, yeh, locked in there . . . but it's still alive . . . Yeh. Let's go.*) Held up to the lights and declared *Still alive* in the Trailways Bus Terminal on Canal Street, New York City, New York, as good a place as any. The time had been 5:55 PM when the disturbance began. The Master Key was summoned, and delivered out of its duffel bag the screaming ungrateful little—

"Bobbie Gotteson" hears the name "Bobbie Gotteson" uttered and a long loud string of words he tries to interrupt, rising to his feet though his legs are weak, interrupting the words to cry "I Bobbie Gotteson being of sound mind and body do hereby request—insist—want—" while the Judge stares and the courtroom goes wild and the bailiffs and the police converge—and the Maniac falls back in his chair— Counsel is advised by someone very angry to instruct his client "Bobbie Gotteson" to refrain from such outbursts this is a Court of Law he is on trial for his life if that can't make him into a sober mature

responsible adult what will?[*]

—screaming ungrateful little red-faced monkeyish diaper-soaked Bobbie Gotteson, delivered to the gawkers out of foot-locker 79-C, already in trouble with the Law. Mouthy little sonuvabitch. Mouth runs away with it though on trial for its life, just as mouth ran away with it at the age of 1 week. Mouth has a sense of humor. Jokes too much. Gets the rest of it into trouble, as the Prosecuting Attorney is going to show in all that detail, the bastard. Public records will show and are never wrong. Public records were following closely and were never wrong causing tax-payers to rebel . . . *What, is it still alive?* *. . . Alive?* Bobbie Gotteson is already there, existing in the typed-up words in the reports and can't be erased or wished away by the friendliest Friends of the Court or the pickets (mainly kids, looking skinnier and uglier and crazier than I do) outside this Hall of Justice, picketing for the release of the Maniac. Mouth might as well confess. Mouth might as well inform on itself.

When the screaming stopped and the diapers were changed the joking started, but jokes only got it into trouble. You wouldn't think so, but it was true. Into trouble and into it deeper and deeper, a total of seventeen years four months fourteen days spent Inside, but with a cheerful natural bright sense of humor and a basic optimism that ebbed or was kicked hard occasionally but always surfaced again. Sheer delight is the Maniac's energy, always bubbling back, the best trick of all as was demonstrated on Variety Night or Talent Show nights, and afterward in the Outside World (which you inhabit not knowing it is Outside of other people's Inside, but more of that later!—later!), but somehow sweetest of all when fellow inmates doubled over with laughter and sometimes had to beg it to stop, *Jesus Bobbie, Jesus kid, cut it out you're killing me—!* What did they like best? Popular opinion divided equally between the *spider-monkey-climbing-up-a-pole* routine and the

[*]One of Gotteson's fixed ideas was that he faced death in the gas chamber, though he had been told repeatedly that capital punishment had been abolished in the State of California. All remarks in this strange document are the Maniac's, even those he attributes to the "court" and to other people.

12

spastic-crossing-the-freeway pantomime. Inmates showed surprising enthusiasm and spontaneous interest in these amateur nights—even the most hardened criminals, even the cruelest and hardest of heart could find a tear, or laugh till tears rolled down their coarse cheeks . . . which only goes to show you . . . doesn't it? . . .But wouldn't you know it, no surprise, that's human nature, after the first flush of excitement and enthusiasm interest in Variety Night or Talent Show Night always faded away, and the hard work, the hard grinding work, had to be done by just a core of prisoners . . . you can't beat human nature, Inside or Out. Hard work to organize rehearsals and paint scenery and fight people off and find a lonely corner somewhere to practice your songs and dance-routines and mimes, so by the time *And now—little Bobbie Gotteson!* summons you out of the wings and onstage you are haggard and weary and must pull yourself up by your own gray wool-and-cotton socks, so to speak, in an effort to appear happy. But I had a natural talent for show business, for pleasing the crowd, I was always singled out for applause and encouraged to express myself by people in uniforms, so as to induce paroxysms of laughter in other people, or maybe a stray tear.

If it please Your Honor and the Ladies and Gentlemen of the Jury my client is quieted down and people can stop snickering and gawking and prodding one another and giggling in the corners . . . and that motherfucker on the bench can stop smirking and trying to catch Bobbie's moist brown eye with a wink . . . and the fact remains as a matter of Public Record that the Maniac was delivered to the world out of Locker 79-C in the main waiting room of the Trailways Bus Terminal on Canal Street New York City, as good a place as any and why are you snickering?—the dark, dark odorous Inside of the locker and the urine-soaked duffel bag were sweet to our Bobbie, as to anyone on the other side of sanity.

2

The Maniac Explains His Sanity

I can play sane, like you. Like everyone. Sometimes I played insane, but now I am very sane. My mind is a net, with holes in it that can be very tiny or quite large; to sift things through or to catch them.

Twice my life was saved by playing insane. The first time, in a jail in Reno on my way out here, I woke up and some old wire-bearded bastard was staring down into my face. His lips were moving. He seemed to see me inside, his eyes were really scooping into mine, and he started mumbling some words about his *little girl.* He grabbed hold of me and tried to embrace me. He said I had a little girl's mouth, that it was *his* little girl, a terrible panic ran everywhere in me and I began to beat him around the face to make him let go of me, but he wouldn't let go, he was shrieking now, and I butted at his face with the top of my head, in a rage, to make him let go of me. *My little girl! My girl!* Like hell I am your little girl, Gotteson raged, Gotteson with his muscles and his chest-hair and his deep bass voice, but when he fell down and grabbed my legs I saw he was hurt bad, there would be trouble, already the sheriff's men were headed for us, so I proceeded to go crazy. It saved me from a beating. I was transferred to a psychiatric ward in a hospital that was very modern, and after a while charges were dropped against me, whatever they were, maybe loitering or vagrancy. I was always an expert actor. At another place where they give you tokens for behaving well, instead of beating you, I acted so well that I accumulated heavy sagging pockets filled with tokens.

Another time my life was saved by playing insane, out here. A contact came to pick me up, in a blue Ferrari, and he told me to leave behind my guitar because it wouldn't be needed tonight. I asked him what was wrong. I asked if the client had changed his mind, if the party was called off, and he said well, no, the client has not changed his mind but the instructions were different from what I had been told. He said, to put on a blindfold he had in the glove compartment. So I put it on. But I took the guitar with me because there wasn't a safe place to leave it, and we drove out somewhere up into the Hills, that was pretty obvious, and I just relaxed and thought well hell, I would just relax and not even make nervous jokes to the man who was driving, but try to sit calmly, and relax. So we stopped somewhere out in the country. He said, O.K., take the blindfold off, it's already past ten and we were due at ten, so we got out and he opened the trunk of the car and took out two leather thongs with fringes on them and a leather arm-band with something propped up on it. I asked him what the hell that was, but he said just to put it on, so I buckled it on my forearm and a car came around a curve just then, so in the headlights I saw that it was a bird pasted onto the arm-band, and it was so strange with its glass eyes and sharp curved beak that I stood staring at it while the car went by, and my friend shouted at me to wake up, or we'd both be in trouble. He had put on a helmet with a feathery fringe to it, going all around the helmet though longer at the sides and the back, and he told me to get going up through the brush and began to explain what the assignment was. We would be told to stop, he said, but we must not even pause—must shout *No mercy! No mercy!*—and keep on beating the client. I began to concentrate my powers inside my head. By the time we smashed our way through a terrace door and into the sunken living room where a man sat watching television I was all on fire and could not have been stopped except by bullets. The stuffed falcon shivered on my arm. The client, seeing my face, began to scream. But there was no stopping me and *no mercy.*

In a frenzy I slashed at the client's bare exposed face and could not hear what people were shouting. A kind of blackness came over me. I seemed to fall through the floor, as if the thick white woolly carpeting of that expensive home vanished and there were coarse floorboards with cracks between them and boards missing in places, through which I fell in my excitement. On all sides I danced and lunged. I was wiry, wily. I was galvanized with energy as if energy shot through me in spasms. . . . And then I was being dragged somewhere, then someone was shouting at me that it was a mistake, we had broken into the wrong house, and I must stop what I was doing. Must stop! Gotteson need never stop, I told him. Why should Gotteson stop once he begins? It is all inertia, a vast mountain slow to begin its upheaval and then hungry to continue, in fact unstoppable. Gotteson showed *no mercy*.

And so I pretended madness, to save myself from disaster. Yet I was always sane. I am like you: a progression of states of mind, forms of sanity that keep moving and eluding definition. I was always sane and had practiced insanity so well that in falling through the floorboards I came upon an earlier wiser self, that seemed to know the way out of that house and had no need for the shouting of my friend. Outside, on the terrace, I was overcome by a flash of certainty, a forward-leaping vision of what I must do—what I had already done, in the future, and only needed to remember now in detail—and I wound the leather thong around my friend's neck in order to strangle him into collapsing, not into absolute death, and so escape. All this was done with calculation, though it took place in two or three minutes—rushed and frenzied and noisy—and I ran back down the hill through the underbrush to safety.

A Maniac is immortal. He cannot be killed except by his own manipulations.

The Courtship of the Spider Monkey

there she is awaiting him
alone in a hole
that is a room
in a house honeycombed
with holes

hand-over-hand he climbs
foot-over-foot up the side of the house
the master of gravity
concentrated as a bridegroom

the Moon and the Machete
communicate with winks

The courtroom is restless. The third juror from the left, in the back row, is staring at the Maniac with a look glistening as the Maniac's. There is something about the Machete that excites us all.

3

The Machete

It sliced up more people than they have records for, how's that for a tease? You think that the State's records show everything?—every slash? There were more brides than I remember. The Machete was, is, two and a half feet long, purchased at an Army-Navy Surplus Store in town here, a blade of steel, a sturdy man-sized handle, nothing like that thing the Prosecution has under its control. *That* blade is dull. If it is stained, the stains are rust and not blood. You can't bring the Spider Monkey's powers into the Hall of Justice; you can't even see the Machete except by moonlight.

Doreen B. waited like a tender space to be threaded, the way you thread a needle. I didn't know her name until the next day, until the newspapers came out.

4

Gotteson's Juvenilia

Poems written at the age of 15, about which
his English teacher at the Vocational High School
in Newark, New Jersey, said "These are
the products of a sick mind, Bobbie."

The Train

a toy train the size of a real train
was stalled in the dark in a field
the temperature on both sides of the glass was 0°
but the passengers were shouting anyway
to get out
they were pounding on the windows
so I drove out with a fireman's ax
to smash the windows and let them loose
but the ax got away from me and flew through the dark
and when it returned to me it was bloody
and there were hairs on it

this taught me to be patient
and wait in the dark

The Cocoon

I was sleeping in the cocoon
stretched out to the exact size of the cocoon
five foot seven and a half inches
I was sleeping there and very happy
then the alarm rang
my foster-brothers ran into the room

my foster-father grabbed me by the ankles
I screamed for him not to pull me down backwards
but he laughed and said "Time to get up!"
they all laughed and dragged me backwards
out of the cocoon

when you are yanked backwards like that
the insides of the cocoon turn to razors
even your eyes are pressed into your head
by the time your head is free
your brain is suffocated
but you get dressed anyway
and go to school anyway
hoping no one will notice

The Food-Chain Blues

when you are inside the package
you can't read the insignia on front
or the magic Date of Expiration
past which you will turn
unhygienic

5

Unrehearsed Interview
With a Child Therapist, Somewhere in Newark

THERAPIST

. . . your mother has issued a complaint, says she had to call the police on you, Bobbie. For shame! What's your explanation this time? Why do you make life so hard for yourself and your family and this office?

BOBBIE

. . . not my family. They're not my family.

THERAPIST

Your father isn't well, it says here. Kidney ailment, eh? Your mother has issued a formal complaint saying that she's at the end of *her rope,* her exact words; she can't handle you and her own children—says all three of you are uncontrollable—

BOBBIE

They promised not to go after me. They said so. I told them I could protect myself. . . . said I'd take them both with me. I could do it. —It wasn't my father; it was my foster-father. It wasn't kidneys that killed him. Somebody backed over him in a—

THERAPIST

. . . Looking through your files is quite a revelation. Quite a revelation! . . . Did poorly on the Wenshler Verbal Skills when you were six . . . I.Q. somewhere between 48 and 78 . . .

Hardison-Radt Abstraction-Perception very, very poor . . .
Faulty development of conceptualizing abilities . . . plus disjointed motor coordination and speech mannerisms. . . .What's
that sniffling? Are you sniffling?

BOBBIE

No. Not me.

THERAPIST

It's obvious that you need love, obvious as the funny pug nose
on your face, eh-heh, but *who* has got the stomach for it . . .
the crucial question of our era. Eh? The last time I fell for that
sniffling trick, my boy, and put my hand out to one of you—a
cute little creature with cartoon freckles and big brown weepy
eyes—the little bastard bit my finger down to the bone, bit right
through the joint and swallowed the fingertip, nail and all.
Here, look at this. How I screamed! What agony! —And for
what? What was accomplished? They offered to stomach-pump
my fingertip out of him and graft it back on me, but *no thanks!*
I didn't even want it back after that disgusting experience. . . .
how to continue as a professional with integrity, a complex
multi-dimensional young man with high ideals, confronted
hourly by meager one-dimensional stereotypes like you. . . . I
want subtlety, is it too much to ask? . . . Your father's dead,
you say? Did you say he's dead?

BOBBIE

It wasn't my father.

THERAPIST

That reminds me, Bobbie, the law requires that you be placed at
all times in a home with both parents living—with both a
mother and a father. So I'm afraid we'll have to move you.

BOBBIE

I'm ready to go.

THERAPIST

It will only take a few weeks to get the papers cleared, and in the meanwhile I can have one of the secretaries type up these forms. . . . Why are you squirming like that? Don't you feel well?

BOBBIE

I'm ready to go. Wherever you people send me. I can pick up and go anywhere. I'm ready. I'm ready all the time—night or day. I don't sleep. I stay awake so I can be ready.

THERAPIST

That's fascinating, Bobbie. And you're only—how old?—this record says you're fourteen, but you look older to me. You look a lot older to me. You're about the hairiest monkey-ugly fourteen-year-old bastard I've seen in a long time, Bobbie. It's pathetic, actually. I think what we'll do is, to take a few short-cuts, just telephone juvenile court and set up a date, and that way your mother can dump you without a lot of red tape. Back you go into the bin! Back for the tax-payers to feed! Yes, it's the same old story. Your original mother dumped you, and the State took you on. Fed you, changed your diapers, educated you, set you up in excellent foster homes, but you can't appreciate it, can you?—with your monkey-ugly little face, that certainly looks as if it needs a shave. Is that the beginning of a beard . . . ? It's obscene, actually, to sit knee-to-knee with a creature like you. You're not human. You don't appreciate what people do for you. Huge taxes go into public education, yet kids like you roam the streets illiterate; you can barely read the street signs and can manage to tell one brand-name of automobile from another only by counting the number of letters. . . .

BOBBIE

I'm ready to go . . . I can go to the next place from here . . . I can walk to it. . . . I've defeated the force of gravity. . . . I can go anywhere.

Uh, yes. It's obvious to our office that you're going to grow up as an institutionalized person, and from the looks of you you'll be involved in a murder in a few years—from the looks of your shoulders and arm muscles *you'll* probably do the strangling, though it could be the other way around if you cross up your sweetheart and he gets angry at you. But I could be mistaken: you could grow up on the Outside. In which case I'm sure you *will* do the murdering yourself. But you won't make a penny out of it. The royalties will go to complete strangers. The starring role in the movie will go—of course—to someone handsomer than you, and of course much taller. You're just too short to be taken seriously. No, you won't make a penny out of it, you'll be famous but back in the bin again, eating out of the tax-payers' hand forever. That's the way it is with little monkey-bastards like you, you just lose. Right? It's a losing game. You can't win. . . . But there's no point in crying about it, or whatever you're doing. That wheezing noise won't change the constitution of the universe, Bobbie. Forget it. I'll get you back in Boys' Home right in the city here and you'll be off the streets and safe for a while from your own evil nature. Will you please stop crying? Don't you have a Kleenex? It's disgusting, actually, to have to witness behavior like yours . . . a man like myself begins with high ideals, goes into graduate school prepared to devote himself to humanity, and what does he end up sitting knee-to-knee with?—little blue-chinned muscle-bound monkey-faced bastards like Bobbie Gadsen . . . or Gotsen . . . or Gotteson, whatever the hell this word is, the typist X'd half the word out. *You're a word that's been half-X'd out, Bobbie!* Poor little bastard!

6

El Portal
The First Night

"I'll just pretend you're not here," she said.

"What should I do?" I said.

She walked away. She turned her back to me. I could see the spine beneath the skin, rippling there, the vertebrae moving like tiny knuckles . . . and the front of her face was slit sideways with a grin, I knew it though I couldn't see it.

"What should I do?" I shouted.

She laughed and walked away. She walked across the terrace. The wind got into her fluffy pale hair and she clutched at it with both hands, helplessly. She turned her body so that the wind moved with it, eased along it. She was laughing. I stared at her and knew what I was expected to do. They were expecting me to do it. She jumped up on the wall—it was a narrow wall made of rock—and walked along on top of it, her arms outstretched as if she were sleepwalking, balancing herself above that fifteen hundred foot drop. She glanced back at me, her eyes narrowed in excitement. The sun was behind a thin tissue of clouds. A rainbow formed and dissolved. She was laughing, her porcelain-white teeth were laughing at me, she cried over her shoulder, "You little monkey!—hairy little honey-monkey!" This made me laugh, against my will. They were watching. They were expecting me to do something. So I ran across the terrace and followed along beside her, while she pranced above me, darting these little mock-loving glances at me, drawing her lips together in a shocked pout, then smiling, then grinning, while behind her things were sailing in the air—circling—constantly circling and looking for food— "Watch out for the buzzards, they might get in your hair," I said. She giggled. I didn't touch her, just to tease her. "They might get in your hair like bats and snarl you all up, tear into you, they might poke out your eyes and that wouldn't be so funny, would it?" I cried. From this angle I could see the thickening flesh around her jaw, she wasn't as young as I had thought, and the flesh of her upper arms was loose, very pale, wobbly, strange. . . . "You should wear more clothes," I said. "You should cover yourself up more. Except your legs, your legs are all right . . . your legs are very nice." She couldn't hear me because of the wind, she paused and cupped her hand to her ear. "Your legs are very nice!" I shouted.

"Louder!" she said, waving over my head. I supposed there was a camera and a sound-track machine behind me. How close were they?—would they use a zoom lens? I danced along beside her, beginning to snatch at her, just picking at her as if I were picking feathers—little pinches of my thumb and forefinger—pinching her thighs, her legs while she giggled and hopped away from me. One of the hawks darted down straight into the water behind us. She screamed, surprised. She jumped down from the wall and into my arms. We staggered backward, laughing. I began to tear at her clothing. It was all open in the back, scooped down to below her waist, and I tore it into pieces while she screamed and tried to get her fingers around my throat. "No you don't, no you don't!" I said.

"I'm not one of your little-girl sluts!" she screamed. "I'm famous! I don't need you! I don't need to be humiliated like this! —Stop that, you little bastard, I'll have you arrested!—stop that!—I said stop that!"

"Your face is slipping to one side," I whispered. "Your mascara is running—"

But she was scratching at me and didn't hear. "Little wop bastard! Little monkey-bastard!"

"I'm not a wop," I said. "I'm an American. —Don't you care, your make-up is all slipping down?"

We wrestled together on the flagstone terrace. She shrieked and tried to roll away from me. I straddled her. "I have a son your age, stop this, I have a son—I have two sons—I don't need you to do this—I'm above this—I— I'll have you put on Death Row!—stop it!—you're diseased, you're sub-human, stop it, my children are here—they're watching—I know they're loose

26

and watching—stop—wait—" I put my hand over her mouth, the gritty dirty palm of my right hand. She tried to wrench away. How we laughed together, secretly!—behind my hand, how we laughed! And the universe grew powerful, every cell of my body leaped with the desire *to do well*, and I—

She got loose and waved wildly back at the house, where they were standing and applauding. She jumped to her feet, but I grabbed hold of her leg at the calf, then at the thigh, and yanked her down again. "Stop him, I'm sick, I'm raw, I'm worn out!" she cried, but they ignored her screams; only the cameraman approached us, barefoot, crooning words that seemed to be addressed to me. I didn't pay attention to them. Found a clump of her blond hair in my fist. "Oh Bobbie, Bobbie, Bobbie you maniac," someone crooned. It might have been the cameraman. It might have been Melva.

Afterward sometime I lay at the shallow end of the pool, utterly still. The pores of my body were now closed. I could hear them inside the house. I thought, *I will close myself from them.* But one eye remained open, sharply, slyly, focussing on Bobbie Gotteson now on film, one of his performances now on film, one of his performances on film at last, though it wasn't the performance Bobbie had hoped to give. But . . . !

Oh Bobbie, Bobbie, Bobbie you handsome monkey, you sweet maniac, oh Bobbie, where did you come from?—what powers do you possess?

7

The Maniac Meditates
Upon His Powers and When They First
Got Him into Trouble

I heard somebody yelling at her in my own voice—it was a boy yelling—a boy maybe eleven or twelve years old—yelling—

Didn't she know, the nasty stinky ugly old bitch, that I could set fire to this place if I wanted to?—could set fire to the stinky place we lived in and the stinky living room sofa where I had to sleep and the stairs and the whole building—didn't she know this simple fact? Didn't she know that I could set fire to her too and she'd go up in smoke, her baggy dresses and her underskirts and underwear all flaming up in smoke, didn't she know—?

Which one of them was this?

One of them, I don't know which one; one of my mothers.

Yes, just listen: I yelled at her (it was some woman grabbing me by the shoulders tough and ready to bite and screaming back into my face) and when that didn't work I whispered starting to sob, didn't she know that I could do anything if I let my mind free?—if I unleashed it to do my secret will? And she just shook me and screamed and banged me against the wall and the radiator and my powers rushed to me, filling out my skinny arms and legs and chest, but she had more power, she had the power of thumping me back against the radiator so my left leg was in terrible pain and I could not get my mind razor-sharp enough to slice sideways through her. ". . . could light fire to you and you'd go up . . ." but nobody gave a damn, but right at that instant the melody of a song shot through my mind . . . and much, much later . . . much later

. . . five or six years later . . . fooling around with a guitar in the Recreation Unit . . . the melody and the complete lyrics of my first song came to me, complete. Do you know it? Does anybody know it? They stole it and changed the words but the words are *Could set fire! to you! and you'd! go up!* and no other words. . . .

I wrote a hundred songs, two hundred, a thousand! . . . People here don't believe me, they hate me. But pals of mine back in the East or out here, and Inside, *they* would not lie . . . would not try to cheat me . . . *they* would vouch for me! That song on the back of the Survivors' hit single, a few months ago, the one they called "Learning to Love"—that's *my* song— you check out the record and see, it's my name down there, *Bobbie Gotteson* right there in the credits. . . . But the bastards cheated me. They cheated me like everybody else cheated me. They took my song and changed the title to that shitty title—*my* song was called "Unlearning to Live" and was a beautiful song—and those bastards, always screwing around and zonked out of their heads half the time, millionaire-bastards, *my own age!*—they bought my song from me for twelve lousy hundred dollars and changed the title and the words and— Melva's son, the bastard is *younger than I am!*— the bastard heard me singing at Lucky Pierre's, that's on the Strip, and hung around and told me how good I was, and—

Then they got an injunction with the police. They tried to defraud me. They tried to curtail my rights as a citizen. I was born in this country like everyone else! *I am an American through and through!* And they got a Jew lawyer to defraud me of my rights, got the Los Angeles Police Department to come move me out of that house—where I was an invited guest— where I was made to understand I could live as long as I wanted to—and my guitar was smashed, a cop smashed it in with his foot, right while I stood there crying and trying to explain to them— "I'm a song-writer," I yelled. "I'm a musician!" The place was all wrecked by them, mattresses lying around and garbage all over, the dead ocelot I had to kill—had to smash its brains in with a lead lamp-stand, when it went crazy one night —the ocelot had started to rot—and I wasn't feeling well, staggering around and trying to wake up, and the bastard cops break the door down and arrest me— "Who are you threatening?" they asked me. "Is your name 'Bobbie Gotteson'? You're under arrest—you're being charged with extortion and felonious assault and trespassing and refusal to vacate the premises of a private establishment—"

I put up my usual fight. I'm a good fighter. I learned in prison to . . . to not give in . . . not to snitch, and not to give in. . . . But they worked me over and when we got to the station I puked all over the stairs going in, and they gave me hell for that, and there was so much vomit and blood I couldn't talk over the telephone . . . trying like crazy to get through to somebody, to get a lawyer, to get a call through to somebody for help. . . . But my mind caved in. So when they said, *Hey boy, you greasy hairy little spic, hey, you going to threaten any more white ladies?*—I got it confused in my mind with being ten or eleven years old, a skinny little freaked-out runt back in New Jersey, with my drunk old lady yelling at me one day in the hall outside where we lived—and—uh—it all got collapsed into itself, the different times, and I was saying to her that I could fire her up and the whole building if I wanted to, if she would just stop screaming, stop screaming!—but that was when she ran for the police, my own mother, and came back with a cop from two blocks away, that was directing traffic out in the middle of a street, and madder than hell, a big, bull-sized Irish bastard, and my mother yelling for everybody in the building to hear, "Arrest him! Arrest him! He threatened my life!"

. . . So the cop said, "Boy, did you threaten this lady's life?"

So I said, "No."

She slapped me and said, "He tried to kill me—he's a born killer!"

The policeman slapped me when I tried to get away. "You tried to kill her? You tried to *kill* her?"

She was breathing so hard it turned into sobbing; then she staggered and pressed her hands against her stomach. The cop knocked me back against the stairway railing. "Got a knife, kid?—huh? You got a weapon? Where is it? Where is your weapon?" He squeezed me. Squeezed my legs up and down. Yanked at my shirt—tore it across one shoulder. His face was red. "Trying to kill people, huh? Off to a good start in life, huh? Little wop!"

8

An Unfilmed Love Scene

The drill bounced against my tooth. An upper back tooth. Everything narrowed to it, it was a little island of crazy bright whining pain, but I sat very straight in the chair with my hands gripping the armrests and my feet flat on the platform, so I wouldn't go crazy and start kicking, but the thing in my mouth . . . it was a hooked plastic thing that caught onto my lower lip and teeth to drain the spit away . . . the thing didn't work right and got crooked, and water dribbled down my chin, and more water with a metallic taste began to form in a puddle at the back of my mouth, so I began to choke and the dentist said, "Hold still or I'll drill right through your cheek—" and there it went again, the whining pain like fire right up into my jaw, screaming like a jet, right up past my jaw and into my head—

"Hold still! Hold still!" cried the dentist. I could smell how he was sweating. He was a fat, angry man, out here at the prison on Wednesdays, with a lot of work to do, and his stomach pressing against my forearm, my forearm was bare, my sleeve was worked up to my elbow somehow with all the tension and pain, and when he paused with the drill I opened my eyes to get some reality, some contact, but the pain dizzied me so I could only see the wavering wiggling lines of pain, out there, in the air. A thing had been yanked down in front of me, with a light shining out of it, right into my eyes. The dentist was muttering to his assistant, a plump soft-looking plain little girl with a pony-tail, "Go get me some . . . hand me that thing . . . what's slowing you down? . . . I've got six more of these to do this afternoon, hurry up! . . . his breath is so foul I may lose my lunch. . . . You're going to have some real trouble, my friend," he said to me, angrily, making the drill buzz against a piece of metal, "just wait till that rot hits your nerve canals! . . . you never brush your teeth, *of course not*, which is why your teeth are green and your blood stream polluted with decay and your gums . . . Jesus Christ, your gums would make a display in a special issue of *Dental News!*—" Here he began drilling again. It was a different drill now, a low rumbling whirring one, very strange, coarse, like a slowed-down saw, and his voice got mixed up with the whirring—"All rot! Rot! *Rot!* They expect us to drill out the rot and get the hole clean and fill it in again with silver, do they, eh?—and all this standing on our feet for eight hours a day five goddam days a week and half a day on Saturday—and who is it for?—it's for criminals, rapists, murderers, and potential sadists, like you, what's-your-name, cringing in the chair—lucky for you this isn't an electric chair, eh?—or maybe it is?—eh?—they say the electric chair gets it over quick, too quick for some of the disgusting bastards who get strapped in it, in my opinion, and in the opinion of a lot of others, frankly, but *this* is one chair where you don't get it over with quickly, is it, my boy? Is it? Hold still! This doesn't hurt and you know it. You're a coward. The last man in here, he fell asleep under the drill—*fell asleep*—because he trusted me, he didn't flinch against me, he didn't set himself in opposition to me the way you are— Betty, hand me that towel. What the hell?—where is this blood coming from? Betty! All right now, sit still, it slipped a little but who's to blame, eh?—with you wiggling all around in the chair like a little weasel—lucky for you my schedule is packed or we'd have to do something about that wisdom tooth on its way down, it looks crooked to me, if the X-ray machine was working we'd get the low-down on that little number!—now this might hurt a little, because the hole is exposed now to the air and—"

I began screaming.

When the screaming stopped I could hear it echoing. The dentist was backing away. "I'm through!" he said. "Call the guard and get the little bastard out of here! I don't have to put up with torture in the line of professional duty—this is going too far—this is an outrage— And my stomach hasn't been right since he came into the room, his breath is an outrage—"

The side of my head by the tooth, the right side, on up and

through the back of my skull it rang with pain, all pounding and fizzing with pain, and inside it someone was yelling at me: "—could puke, the creatures I have to treat!—could keel over and *puke*—and now he's got an exposed root and it serves him right, let him feel some human pain for a change, instead of stinking up the place with his pyorrhea and his armpits—the little ape!—if the tax-payers of this state could peek in the door here and *see* just what their money is being poured into, the kind of rat-hole their money is being poured into—"

The girl helped me out into another room. I staggered, I couldn't see right. My eyes were filled with tears. Another prisoner on his way in gaped at me and said, "Jesus Christ . . ." and whimpered, and the girl let me sit down for a minute because my knees felt wobbly. She said something to me but I couldn't hear. I was hunched over, both hands pressed against my jaw. The girl was standing over me, wringing her hands the way one of my mothers did. She was saying, "Aw heck, hey, don't cry—hey—hey, your name is Bobbie, ain't it?—Bobbie?" She came around to face me, squatting down. She stared up into my face where my eyes were out of focus. Her thighs stretched the white material of her dress; the skin of her throat and her face was so soft, so soft-looking, one touch would mar it, one poke of a finger would destroy it, her lips were pink with lipstick and were murmuring words I should be hearing. . . . "That wasn't fair of him, I saw what he did, he didn't freeze your gum and that was a dirty trick . . . just to save a few minutes, so he can get out of here faster. . . . And that wasn't true, what he said about some guy falling asleep in the chair, well, that was a lie, it happened back in town with his own practice and the guy never fell *asleep* but had a heart attack or a stroke or something and had to be carried out feet first. . . . I don't know why he tells such lies, right in front of me! I hate him! I should report him for drilling you without Novocain, on purpose to torture you, then see how he likes it!" She shook her head angrily. Tears came loose in her eyes. A tear rolled down her cheek. She was my age, sixteen or seventeen.

But I hated women. On principle.

One of the exhibits is the Defendant's notebook of "obscene drawings." They are mainly circles meant to represent the female body. The circular parts are drawn lightly and sloppily, the other parts—the holes and slashes—are filled in brutally, angrily, blackly, and it is obvious that the Defendant broke the point of his pencil sometimes while drawing these things— When the notebook is shown to the jury, all the jurors gasp and look away, men and women both. It is shocking, and saddening, to see the graphic workings of a sick mind.

My Old Man up at that prison taught me how to hate them. Hate hate hate hate hate hate hate *hate* them Bobbie. Baby Bobbie. "Baby Bobbie Gotteson" was one of my names. My Old Man's name was Danny Minx also known as Danny Blecher and he warned me, he whispered in my ear in his meaty hot breath-warning, just a friendly warning, "If you even think about them, Baby Bobbie, I'll cut off your balls. How's that?"

9

Unfilmed Love Scene
In the Back Seat of Melva's Rolls-Royce

"You hate me, don't you? You hate women, don't you? Oh you think you can trick me, squirming and writhing and groaning like that, you're all alike, *you all share a filthy little secret!* Bobbie! Stop or I'll roll down the window and scream for help! Bobbie, this is not the place—this isn't the place—"

"Yes. Yes. Yes, it's the place," I said, from the back of my mouth, where the darkest sourest spit was gathering, and I scrambled all over her and thrust my knuckles in her mouth to quiet her because it was what came next; my head was just open and receiving that day, and all that remained of Bobbie Gotteson was the black poison at the back of my mouth that I had to swallow so I wouldn't spit it into her face, Bobbie in a dark red monkey-outfit with gold buttons and braid, selected from a Novelty & Costume Shop on Sunset Boulevard, by Melva herself, just the right uniform for a five-foot-seven-and-a-half-inch chauffeur with black curly wiry hair and black curly wiry chest hair (showing at the top of his coat, where the first three buttons are unbuttoned) who has been waiting for two and a half hours for his mistress to appear. Melva then did appear, making her way through the shoppers and tourists on the street, her hair now bone-white and not puffed out any longer but arranged in stacks like a wedding cake, little curls all around her forehead and hiding her ears, and in spite of the two and a half hours she'd spent in the beauty parlor I knew it was necessary for me to scramble over the seat and cover her with love-pecks, pouting puffed-up motions of my mouth, so that passers-by had something to see, even if this wasn't being filmed. Melva screamed. The car windows were up, the air-conditioning on, no one could hear her or if they could hear it wouldn't matter, I had the impression out of the corner of my eye that someone was even taking a snapshot of us—though I might have been mistaken—though Melva had the idea those days that one of her sons was following us around, jealously, and had put a staple into the front left wheel of the car so that the air dribbled out of it slowly and left it flat, for us to discover when we emerged from our bungalow at San Luis Obispo one morning. *Bobbie, my precious Bobbie, my brutal little Bobbie-glutton, wait till you get in show business—how proud I'll be, how the public will devour you!—just wait!* Melva teased me with the promise of a screen-test and a recording session, she whispered that she had a contact in Vanbrugh's studios, she knew all the executives there, then she whispered one night that she knew Vanbrugh himself, and in fact was an "ex-associate" of Vanbrugh's, she called him Vannie, and snuggled against me murmuring *Vannie, Vannie, all of you are alike, sweet Bobbie-Vannie, you could be a son of his, you could be one of my own darling boys . . . maybe I'll adopt you, tuck you under my wing and into my will!—maybe maybe maybe maybe—*

I wanted to rip the eyelids off her. First the left. Then the right. Frosted-silver eyelids.

A pool gathered at the back of my mouth. Poison leaking out of my gums, maybe. Greenish-black martini-sour liquid. On the pillowcases in the morning there were black streaks—but it was Melva's mascara, not my spittle.

"Oh you tried to kill me. You tried to strangle me," Melva sighed.

"Why not?"

"Oh you're getting like all of them, they go downhill one step at a time . . . nastier, filthier . . . more demanding. . . . I hardly know my own sons any longer," Melva yawned. She shook her head and smiled vaguely at me. The drug was taking effect. Her marred face, her sagging throat. "But I don't mind. I'm tolerant of different personality types. You wouldn't believe it . . . but back in the '30's I was a member of . . . of . . . of the *Communist Party* out here, and I learned to tolerate everything. But don't ever tell Mr. Vanbrugh on me," she whispered. "If he found out he'd disown me."

I pretended to sleep. It was easier.

"I don't want to be disowned by anyone," Melva yawned. The violence of her yawn ran through both of us. She lay curled against me, her arms around my head so that my face was loosely pressed against her throat, and we were somewhere near the surf, the pounding of the great ocean I had crossed this continent to see, or maybe we were huddled together in the back seat of the Rolls, parked there on the Boulevard amid the rocking thudding thumping rattling noise of cars and buses and strangers who gawked in at us. They too had crossed the great continent. To see. To stare. To take pictures of people like me. Half a block away was a famous restaurant humped like a hat, a brown hat, and if I raised myself on one stiff elbow I might be able to see if one of her boys was hanging out there, by the doorman who was supposed to be—how did I know this?—one of Melva's ex-lovers. The boys took turns spying on us.

10

How the Maniac Gotteson
Travelled West

I wasn't a maniac then. But it took me 21 months to get here.

When they let me out I took a job with a construction company in South Amboy, to wait for my Old Man to get free. He was up for parole in a few months. He said to keep out of trouble, Bobbie, or else—!—and sent word to a contact of his on the Outside to watch me, and to report back to him if I got in trouble; so between the contact who was invisible and my parole officer I knew it was wisest to keep out of trouble. *But I couldn't tell them apart!* My Old Man Danny Minx floated everywhere, invisible, and in jail he'd taught me the powers of the mind and how he sent himself out of his body at will, to roam the streets of the city and be back in time for wake-up at seven, to slip into his body and fool everyone. I don't know. Danny took me under his wing and protected me, so if he was lying or crazy or putting me on I didn't ask questions not even silently, for fear he could read minds. The link between us was very strong, but it ran from him to me and not the other way. I could get messages from him, but couldn't send any. One day hauling lumber at work I got a crisp startling message from Danny to *pursue my musical career.*

So I took guitar and singing lessons from a Spaniard who ran a music shop in downtown Amboy, $1 a lesson and I tried to get in for two lessons a week, to surprise Danny when he got out.

I hummed songs out of the air. I could "receive" words if I hit upon the right tunes. I asked the Spaniard, a little nervous guy, if that was how genius worked—he said it sure was—it *sure was.* One Saturday afternoon, he had me play the guitar for people browsing around the store, like a wandering minstrel, I strummed the chords I knew and wasn't too scared and sang whatever came into my head—

> o you're eatable
> non-repeatable!

—and one silvery-haired man in his thirties or forties asked me for my autograph and to have coffee with him, but he looked so anxious I knew it was more than just coffee he wanted, so I said no. My Old Man would kill me. He had already fucked me in front of two other guys to punish me. At such times he said he was from the "F.B.I." and would "take no sass!"

Danny Minx got out and broke parole to escape to the West, and the two of us drove out together. It took us a long time. I picked up a very fine, new, tight-handling Pontiac, that was parked on a residential street with the keys in the ignition, and in fact still swaying a little in the ignition, since the lady had just jumped out of the car to run into the house. She was sure on her way back again, so little Bobbie acted fast, and in an hour we were many miles to the west of that scene, laughing and treating ourselves to handfuls of chocolates. Danny Minx also known as Danny Blecher said that chocolate was the greatest potion and he had to eat a certain quantity of it every day for medical reasons, to keep his blood sugar level up. It was directly connected with male potency, he said, and I have always found this to be true.

Somewhere just the other side of Wichita the trouble began with Danny, who was forty years old or more, when he stopped to give two college kids a ride. They were boys with short hair and smiles and a sign that said *Going West?* They got in the back seat and the four of us chatted for a while, then Danny giggled and said, "You two wouldn't care to aid and abet a thief, would you?—in pursuit of his daily worship?" The kids laughed a little but didn't catch on. I looked over at Danny where he was grinning. He didn't glance at me. He offered a drink from a bottle of Muscatel and they took the bottle, but I could tell they didn't drink from it, one of them made a swiping motion with his hand as if to wipe the top of the neck clean, and

39

the other giggled, but Danny kept saying certain things to them that they didn't catch onto, until finally I began to shout.

"I'll kill you! You know I can kill you! I can kill you!" I shouted.

Danny began to laugh.

"I can kill everybody! I don't need you! I don't need anybody!"

I shouted and began to pound the seat between us. I was wearing just jeans and a T-shirt and my forearms were thick with curly black hairs that scared the kids in the back seat, I could tell, and Danny glanced down at my hands with that sly sideways look of his, but I wasn't going to be silenced, and for the first time certain things broke free in my mind—shapes and thicknesses—like snarling dogs, bounding and jumping around —and Danny's head jerked back as if he'd been bitten by one of them. He began to talk me down. He began to sing a little song only known to the two of us, in fact it was my own song that I told him was dedicated to him, *you're eatable . . . non-repeatable. . . .*

That song was stolen from me by a two-bit composer at Vanbrugh Studios. It is the background music to one of their movies. They stole everything from me and kicked me out and set their guard-dogs on me, but if Danny Minx could come forth to testify . . . to be a character witness . . . it would be made clear to the public how I was defrauded . . . my talents exploited. . . . "Eatable" is the background music to *Walking Ragged* but there are no credits attached to it, nowhere in the credits does it say "Bobbie Gotteson'. . . .

Did I journey so far West, all the way across this country, only to be fucked on film?

The boys got frightened and said, let us out, and Danny speeded up just for a laugh, and the boys—*college boys!*— began almost to cry and wheedle and I leaned over the seat to shout in their faces. I don't remember what I shouted. I tore at them, lunged back and tried to get hold of their hair so as to bounce their heads together. Finally Danny was laughing so hard he had to stop, and the kids got out of the car and ran away, and left behind some books and a cardboard suitcase, and we sped off again with me yelling out the side window.

Later on I woke up and Danny was parked in a gas station.

The attendant was a kid my age. Danny and the kid were talking about something, I heard a funny whine—like a hillbilly accent—and realized we were out West. I got out of the car. My legs felt strange. My whole body was stiff, my shoulders and chest felt tight, like armor, and my leg-muscles felt all bunched up. I couldn't remember what was going on. I think that was the newness of my powers, the fear of them I had then because I was just a kid, the way my mind could seize hold of reality and give a shape to it, to mold other people to my will; I wasn't used to it yet. I felt very tentative. Danny and the boy stopped talking and looked at me. In those days my hair wasn't as long and thick and curly as it was later, when I got into private films and private catering to parties, when the styles in male fashions had changed, but anyway my black curly hair was eye-catching and I knew it and except for a bluish rough haze around the lower part of my face and going up almost to my eyes, from not shaving often enough, I was very handsome. It made me self-conscious. I walked past Danny without giving him a sign . . . and around behind the garage where there was a Men's Room . . . and when I came out I felt so good, so happy, I crossed a field adjacent to the garage and strolled up to someone's back yard. . . . This was in Colorado, in the eastern part of the state. I don't know how I know this. The sky was bright blue, the clouds were just at the horizon, there were three or four little one-storey houses along a dirt road, clap-board houses, like shanties, and in the back of one of them a little girl was playing . . . playing with, uh, I think it was a doll . . . a naked doll . . . holding onto the legs and fooling around with it in the dirt. . . . It was a little girl, I don't know how old. Two years old? Three? Suddenly I thought of how my powers, if unleashed, could rush out into that child and destroy her. She didn't see me. She had red hair, she was a little thing sitting in the dirt, fooling around. The day was very still. No, a dog was barking somewhere. Out on the highway a truck rumbled past. So powerful! So powerful! I felt the need to discharge my energies, I felt the building-up of powers that would make my skull go out of shape. I stared at the girl. Now she noticed me— she had felt my thought-waves! She left off hitting the doll against the ground and stared at me, and in that instant I felt my powers rise and flow over, like light if light could turn into water, fountains of water, rising and flowing over with love, because the little girl and I were looking at each other in that way, at that time. It happened *at that time.* Another moment, another heartbeat, and it would have been something else and maybe my powers would have killed her. But not *at that time.*

Danny came to get me. He said, "Hey Bobbie, why are you crying?"

I didn't know I was crying, I said.

" Bobbie, honey," he said. "Why hell! Are you crying because I teased you back there? Because of those plain, pimply-faced boys?"

I'm not crying, I said. I seemed to wake up. The back yard was empty, the sky was changed. Two dogs were barking.

Danny stared at me.

We drove on and stopped late in the afternoon for food, and pulled off the highway and down a farmer's lane that led by a railroad track, the car bumping along, weeds scraping against the fenders. Danny made cheese-spread sandwiches for both of us. We sat out in the grass. I knew something was wrong but didn't let on. Danny offered me some chocolates but I had no appetite. Then we both stopped eating and there was a noise somewhere like a train whistle or a coyote, and it made me shiver, because Danny was looking away from me and not directly at me, smiling dreamily at me, the way he always did this time of day. He cleared his throat. I remember exactly the words he said; he said, "Pretend you're in a movie, pretend you're a cowboy singing on the prairie." So I got my guitar out of the back seat of the car. I strummed a few chords and walked along, and began to sing, humming a tune until the words came out of the air to me . . . or maybe they came out of Danny's mind and into mine. . . .

I heard him start the car. But I didn't turn around.

I had enough time to run back to the car, but I didn't. I didn't turn around. It was not the gun Danny carried that stopped me, either. That would not have stopped me. I don't know. I just kept walking along by the railroad track, which was raised maybe three or four feet from the ground, strumming the guitar, singing under my breath. . . . I heard him start the car and back out. But I didn't turn around.

I got to the next town, then to a town after that. Then I got a ride all the way to Reno, where my luck gave out and I was arrested for vagrancy, because they were "cracking down" on drifters in that city. From there I got shipped to a mental hospital, where I made friends with a lady therapist who liked me, and it wasn't until I was released from the Nevada State Hospital and got all the way to Los Angeles that I found out that the President had been assassinated while I was locked up—by a maniac named Oswald, a two-bit punk who I was glad had been gunned down. That punk! That cheap Commie coward! I got hold of a picture of Oswald being gunned down, his face screwed up into a yell, him doubled over with his hands pressed against his stomach, and a sheriff's man starting forward to interfere with Jack Ruby—but finally I had to get rid of the picture because it made me so angry. *It made me want to kill someone.* I worked in Venice Beach for a while, just enough to finance my musical career, composing ballads in my head— "The Ballad of Jack Ruby" was one of them, but it wasn't one of my best songs—and wondered if Danny Minx would ever show up. I would have forgiven him.

He never came.

Or if he did, he had changed. His face had gotten fatter, his chest had gotten wobbly as a woman's. His legs thicker. His voice shrill and cute, saying "Bobbie-this, Bobbie-that," and never letting me alone. Sometimes they followed me around, old guys, applauding when I finished a song and asking for a lock of my hair, asking for my autograph, pretending I was a star—and then kids followed me around also, mostly teenaged girls with long straight hair and big, moronic eyes, all in love with me. I saved money by sleeping on the beach at night. Sometimes in alleys or in doorways. I could sleep sitting up on a park bench and sometimes even with my eyes half-opened, in case a cop noticed me. Then one night in a bar in Venice there was a fight and somebody grabbed me, and the two of us fell and rolled over and over trying to smash each other's head against the floor, a stranger, a maniac I had never seen before, and when things got straightened out I was being booked for attempted homicide and my life caved in on me, and the Legal Aid man said to plead guilty because I had a record and what's the use?—so I pleaded guilty and the judge put me down for 15 years, without looking at me except a quick darting look that made his face squinch up as if he were about to sneeze. I wanted to explain that I was a musician and a troubadour and that my life was meant to entertain, just to entertain people like him, that I had a strong original talent that must be set free . . . it *must* be set free. . . .

"Next case! Get that man out of here!"

"Your Honor—"

"Next!"

"Your Honor, please allow me to sing for you—"

"Get that creature out of here!"

11

Are You in Love

With Someone Who's Not in Love with You . . . ?

About love they were never wrong, the old song-writers, the old commercial millionaire sons of bitches, most of them dead or dying off now in the Seventies and their mansions taken over by kids in their twenties. . . . But they knew. They knew how it was. You love someone and he will not love you. He will love someone else. But that someone else will *not* love him. That someone else might even love you—! Or someone who looks like you. Gotteson was an original so hot-dark in the face, smouldering sullen gleaming glittering dark brown eyes, side-burns of black tough curly hair that inched down, down, down his muscular cheeks as the years went by and the Outside styles approximated the Inside spirit . . . just a few inches too short, so that even his three-inch cork-heeled fancy Italian shoes didn't help, during the brief time he wore them, clonking around town. *Why was he born so short!* But his legs were muscular, hard, they didn't seem to be made of flesh like other men's— *Bobbie, you are so strong!*—and his shoulder muscles were bulging on that trim, tight torso, though he did only fifteen-twenty minutes of vigorous American push-ups every day. His secret was not in his body. In fact, he scorned the body. He *scorned* it. Gotteson made love to the spirit, he sang his melancholy-cheerful ballads to the spirit, and that was why inmates (during Amateur Nights) rolled their eyes and made sucking motions with their mouths, while he performed, those long-drawn-out years at Terminal Island. And when he was Outside, when he walked out with several ten-dollar bills and two changes of clothes, he saw with amazement that the world had caught up with him . . . all the dreams had caught up with him . . . maybe gone a little ahead of him, due to faulty development of conceptualizing abilities and disjointed motor coordination. . . .

Twenty minutes after he had been released from prison, on the bus to Los Angeles, *on that very bus*, a small-boned lanky-haired knobby-kneed girl of about fourteen eased into the seat beside him, sighing, shaking her hair out of her eyes, glancing sideways at Bobbie with that half-startled half-cunning look they all gave him, and murmured something he could not quite hear. Gotteson, unused to the world, to the rattling of the bus and the rapid motion outside the windows, unused to so many people who were free, freely moving about the streets walking wherever they wished, and especially unused to the feverish smell of this young glittering creature, could not comprehend her words. He didn't dare ask her to repeat them. Bobbie and the girl stared at each other. Finally the girl said, smiling: ". . . running away, it's my first time. How about you? They tried to fuck my mind. Back there."

Bobbie cupped his hand to his ear. "Huh?"

"Back there. Back home in Del Mar. Tried to fuck my mind. You know. What about you?"

What about Bobbie?

He feared her and could not believe her yet she pressed into his sweaty innocent palm something she called *sweetheart-greenies*, capsules she and Bobbie took together, to initiate a small friendship.

Yes, they loved him. He was never to blame. They cringed and writhed for him, they squealed, pressed themselves against him accidentally in crowds at Venice Park or in big jumbled weekend streams of tourists and lower-class suburban sightseers along the Strip, couldn't get enough of him. Gotteson had to learn quickly to harden his heart against that horde, or his singing-potency would have been decimated years ago. . . . He hated them. Hate hate hate hate hate hated them. No not all of them, but most of them—*sweetheart-greenies* wouldn't blur the image sufficiently because the terrible truth was that, inside the *hate*, like a tiny perfumy current making its way slyly up through an enormous gaseous poison, was something like *pity*. He knew them from the inside. He was crucified on the cross of his pity for females. . . .

Had he not pitied Melva's whimpering, had he not stuffed

his muscular arms repeatedly into that monkey-jacket just for laughs, I, Bobbie Gotteson, of sound mind though broken body, would not be trying myself for my life, beyond all the reaches legal and extra-legal of the Law: my life would not be this disjointed confession, but a series of haunting melodies joined to lyric language. But no. The love of human beings does us in. We falter, stumble, stoop over, steal fire for them and are punished, mocked, picked to death by tiny painted nails, ooooh'd and aaaah'd over by tiny button-like lips. From the tiny green capsules Gotteson was drawn, by one creature after another, into excursions of the brain beyond all his ability to recall. *Cranks, peps, cartwheels, coast-to-coasts, uppers, black beauties, turnabouts, bennies, dexies, footballs, purple hearts, double-entries, toads, icebergs* . . . and more and more medicine; but such belongs to pathology and we are concerned with art.

Love did him in, does us all in. This includes Doreen B. who never saw him before, was a total stranger to him and he to her, before those tangled shrieking five-and-a-half minutes of his hacking her "to death" (as the papers express it, not knowing that all deaths are suicide, especially newspaper deaths). Sorry sorry sorry sorry. This includes as well Sharleen M. who will not testify against Bobbie in spite of the Prosecution's sly plans. *Never.* They gloat, whisper among themselves, prepare their useless strategies . . . the District Attorney visits her in hiding strokes her baby-blank face and her long hair and woos her famous mama and papa and keeps telling them *All is well, the State of California will triumph!* Will it, eh? Will it? Mama and Papa M. are not exactly the parents of Baby Sharleen; Mama is the mother, but Papa the step-father, third in a series. The original Papa is in France making a movie, or at least that's what Sharleen told everyone, though everyone told *me,* giggling, that this Papa was in a mental hospital right here in town. But Sharleen is not going to testify and it is useless for the Prosecution to gloat over her. She will not testify against her beloved Bobbie Gotteson.*

*Though Gotteson wrote these ominous words 18 days before the news of this tragic child's suicide was released, he seems to have been absolutely certain she would not testify. Readers are not invited to speculate on the true identity of this child, though the "Mama" referred to has obviously made no effort to disguise her involvement with Bobbie Gotteson.

At Terminal Island, Bobbie could have been an Old Man to any number of guidance-craving kids, but his spirit always yearned upward, he desired only men twenty or more years his senior, gentlemanly men but not too gentlemanly, tough-voiced men who were yet elegant, like that Judge who put him away for so many years. Exactly like that Judge! He composed songs for them, secretly. For them. For abrasive-eyed cynical-mouthed gentlemen with class, like Vanbrugh himself, though Bobbie only crept into the presence of Vanbrugh once . . . or into the presence of someone said to be the great Vanbrugh. Even now, melancholy-cunning, he is composing this jokey confession mainly to win the heart of the Judge who will sit above him, glancing at him or not glancing at him, smooth-shaven, cold, deathly, deathly-smiling when it is necessary to smile, a gentleman, a graduate of a Law School whose very name would be so foreign to the Maniac that it would send him into a trance. . . . Gotteson's personal tragedy, in contrast with his professional-social-artistic tragedy, was that the gentlemen with class who glanced at him and then *gazed at him* with immense interest were never the gentlemen he, Gotteson, gave a damn about. It was the others he yearned for. Women, all women, any-age-women stared at Gotteson and in a matter of seconds sank into a kind of open-eyed trance, sometimes offensive to him (even a maniac has some moral values), but sometimes exciting, for despite his aesthetic distaste for females his body often acted on its own . . . perhaps cynically? . . . perhaps with a sense of humor . . . ? But in his deepest clearest soul Gotteson could never never once not even once cajole his intellect into taking any of these females seriously. The one who died beside him and whom he did not abandon, she alone whom he did not abandon in her death, breathing bleeding herself out into the bedclothes, was not truly female at that moment . . . not female, not trapped in being a female . . . in *that.* She had been, like Gotteson himself, a creature of pure . . . pure. . . .

But of that revelation Gotteson cannot speak.

So his tragedy was that he loved people who did not love him. We call that *irony.* And, conversely, he was contemptuous of people who loved him, especially those who crowded and lunged and pawed. . . . In Gotteson's heyday on the Strip, when he strummed his battered old guitar and sang wildly-ecstatically into the sweet dark smoke of Lucky Pierre's, among his fans there were even intellectuals hungering for him. . . . Disguised in out-of-date hippie costumes, their prescription-lens aviator-sunglasses sliding down their perspiring noses, saliva oozing into their square-cut rakish beards, men of middle-age drove long distances to wonder at Gotteson's talent, revealing themselves clumsily but charmingly, in as much privacy as Gotteson allowed, as professors . . . their interest in him only academic of course, of course . . . though one, quite at a disadvantage in the clutter of Lucky Pierre's, wept and pawed at Gotteson, *Why did I spend my years with Jane Austen, my God why, now it's too late*, passed out on the dancefloor, a pity. Good graying still-trim men from the great institutions up and down the Coast, Santa Barbara, Santa Cruz, Berkeley, Palo Alto, San Jose, Riverside, Stockton and Westwood alike. . . . But though they hungered for Gotteson he did not care for them; he disdained neurotics.

Why is love so elusive, so hard-to-come-by? Melva often glared and pouted, a winsome grimace out of a 1946 movie of hers that (according to a woman-friend) had almost *but* not quite won her an Academy Award . . . in a novocaine-frigid lisp declaring: "Why anyone in her right senses should fall in love with a motherfucker like you is incomprehensible. Almost a joke. Sickening, actually. I don't know what civilization is sliding into." Propped up in bed, she sometimes read and reread old *New Yorkers*, kept in messy piles beneath the enormous gaily-canopied bed, as if she sought, there, in the decades-old cartoons and the chaste harmless smudgeless columns of print and advertisements for Tiffany knick-knacks, some coherent explanation for *what went wrong*. When most rattled, Melva sought coherence; and she wanted it gracefully worded. *What went wrong with an entire culture!—a beautiful gracious sane sensible non-syphilitic subscribed-to invested-in way of life!* But in the end as always she would giggle and toss the rumpled old magazines back beneath the bed and snap her fingers for her Bobbie, as always. *O you beast!*

At this point the courtroom lights are dimmed. The fifteen-foot-high windows are covered with canvases to shut out light. The

Prosecution—the District Attorney himself and two youngish ambitious assistants—now cause to be shown to the cleared courtroom that notorious underground classic "17 Mannequins & a Guy," said film purchased by the District Attorney's office through a secret series of negotiations with the director who filmed it (at El Portal, though background shots that might identify El Portal have been carefully blurred or blacked out), a director of international fame whose works have won awards at film festivals everywhere—Nice, Rome, New York City—but whose name is strangely missing from the credits. In fact—there are no credits! Not even the star, Bobbie Gotteson himself, is given screen credit and was certainly cheated of payment for his exhaustive work in the film as its central character, its musical director (the guitar-playing in the background is entirely his), and its inventor (though no film script as such was ever committed to paper); but it is no coincidence that the film's value sky-rocketed after the arrest of Gotteson, from a paltry $500-a-night rental fee to the undisclosed fee which the District Attorney obviously paid into the Liberated Arts Talent Agency that handled the film. . . . No coincidence, and yet Gotteson never got royalties, must sit stricken with shame and rage in the courtroom and witness his own public degradation, see there on the portable screen his handsome swarthy face and body going through its performance for an audience of people who can only gasp, snicker, wheeze, mutter "Oh my God—" or "Stop it!" but in no case, not in a single isolated case, give credit where credit is due and ease the Maniac's frayed nerves with a round of applause! The film runs for only 18 minutes (one minute to each of the dressmaker's dummies and a half-minute at start and finish for artistic zooming shots) yet by the conclusion the Maniac is weeping with exhaustion and despair. The Defense Counsel, sitting stonily beside him, inches his chair a little away from the Maniac. Gotteson weeps in his isolation, inside his vacuum, where he has always wept and where no one filmed him. And if he had been filmed, if his private spiritual life had been committed to film, it would have been his usual luck to be handed merely a cash payment of $700 and a few free meals and someone's year-old car . . . !

The District Attorney, flush-faced, strides before the jury
d has no need to shout now, since everyone is hushed and
lpitating and dare not look into anyone else's face; he has
ly to go through his rehearsed phony-understated routine
d call their attention to the *inhuman monstrousness* of that
havior, the *inhuman energy* of that behavior, the *inhuman
gravity* recorded there . . . and especially to that sword
elded by the actor in the last half of the film, the very
chete here in the courtroom, *the murder weapon itself!* "The
used seemed to go into a trance, seemed to swing into a . . .
at shall we call it? . . ." (and here a phony eyebrow-
tching pause, during which the Maniac wants to scream but
nages to sit rigid) ". . . a sword dance, a fertility-rite-
ting-dance, so bizarre as to make us doubt our senses, and
cene beyond any human ability to fathom. . . . You saw,
es and gentlemen of the jury, how viciously the accused
ked that last mannequin to death—I mean, to pieces? You
? You could not fail to *see?*"

One of the lady jurors is weeping into a handkerchief. The
leman beside her, sweaty-faced, offers to lend her assist-
e, but is rebuffed, and blushes violently. The heaviest juror,
rly young man with sideburns nearly as long and twiney as
Maniac's used to be, before his arrest, is breathing so
rily, his fat chest rising and falling so laboriously, that it
is for a while he may have a seizure of some sort. He closes
eyes; droplets of perspiration run down his face.

The District Attorney strides to the Exhibit Table, seizes
nachete itself, and swings it around him with a violence
nakes people gasp, though the Maniac is contemptuous of
nachete, that piece of metal, knowing that it bears only the
est resemblance to his magical weapon. *He could never use
way I did*, the Maniac whispers into his attorney's ear,
vhen his attorney edges away an inch or two, not looking
n, the Maniac says fiercely, *and neither could you!—or
ne else!*

51

12

Gotteson on Film

A legitimate film-test did take place. It took place at the Vanbrugh Studios. Gotteson was invited to play the guitar and to sing as many of his compositions as he chose, and everyone in the studio congratulated him afterward, *everyone*, though no witnesses can be assembled now to testify that this screen-test did take place and of course the film has been either destroyed or sold as a collector's item to some wealthy Hollywood Hills connoisseur of the arts, name undisclosed . . . without a penny of the profits going to Gotteson.

Ten or eleven or twelve films, no-rehearsal films, partying-films, some of them made when I didn't even know someone had a camera, one of them a joked-up version of that commercial for potato chips that has all the camels and the Rajah with a sword, and one of them a hit-off from a 1939 Dracula movie Sonya C. showed at a party at her house, and oh God it all came back to me in Hermosa Beach where my own bride bled to death beside me and couldn't even say out loud how she loved me or forgave me, it flicked back to me like a playing-card, just the way Dracula what's-his-name sobbed because his true bride died, and left him, that was how I sobbed too but nobody filmed that.

But. . . .

But there *was* a real screen-test. They swore it was real. They were very nice to me, asking after my health, they were very polite and thoughtful, and Vlad J. seemed to be impressed with my performance. He promised that he would *personally* screen it for Mr. Vanbrugh as soon as possible. That screen-test did take place. And now if only . . . if only someone would come forth with it, if only it could be located, if only a group of directors and movie producers and people in the industry would acknowledge, publicly, maybe even sign a petition to be published in the newspapers, that the boy did have talent and might have become a Star, yes, a Superstar, if moneyed interests and circumstances had only favored him! Otherwise Gotteson's private hopes will go down in history as *hallucinations.*

13

Why I Hacked
Nine Women to Death

The "hacking" was only physical and incidental. Don't ask me about the "hacking"!—my body took over, and when bodies take over the spirit sails over the horizon. Pounding, plunging, plummeting, fucking, hacking, what had it to do with *Bobbie Gotteson*, who existed in the realm of spirit? I didn't kill them alone, either, but had disciples to help me, every blood-splattered exhausting moment. The stewardess who crawled under the sofa to observe me was *not* hallucinating when she said there were three or four or five of me, bounding everywhere around the room. She was correct. My disciples sprang out of my head when I willed them into birth, they sprang fully-formed though not all of them were my size or age (in age they ranged from nine or ten years old up to twenty-five or thereabouts), and not all of them were equipped with machetes. The smallest and puniest of my disciples, a boy who bore only a coarse resemblance to me as a child, had to tear into his victim with a dime-store jack knife. That accounts for the confusion about "weapons." It explains why the witnesses who saw me depart from the bungalow saw *one man* (swarthy, about thirty years of age, 150 pounds, dressed in white trousers and a red-and-white polka dot shirt—an outfit belonging to one of the girls) while the surviving stewardess saw *a number of men.*

But all that is bodily, messy, disgusting. I don't care for that part of it myself. The various messes of the human body, though natural enough, have always caused me to cringe and reach for my guitar, in order to transcend physical distress. Atop a rumpled stained bed I have been known to compose an original ballad, swiftly, flicking my hair out of my eyes and strumming wildly in order to transcend the field of battle. *Bobbie, you are so beautiful!* some of them cried.

So it wasn't bodily. No. It was spiritual. The great moment was the one in which I felt my opponent's ego collapse, . . . I *felt* it, though each time was quite different from the others. In some it was the gentle sighing-out of a soul through the mouth . . . in others it was the popping of a tough, stubborn structure, like a plastic bubble . . . and though I did not inflict destructive harm to the actress Irma R. that night at El Portal, I felt the *click!* of her ego as it broke . . . it was no surprise to me when I learned, a few weeks later, that she had died in a sixteen-car smash-up on the Santa Monica Freeway, initiated by Irma herself when her car swayed a few inches to the left as she drove at eighty miles an hour. It wasn't just women, either, though their egos were of course joyous things to smash, but men here and there throughout my life, who died in my arms or before my eyes without shedding blood, without the loss of a heartbeat, but who died nevertheless as Gotteson's ego soared. They gathered themselves together, adjusted their clothing, wiped their foreheads—and walked away! Yet their souls had been smashed, smashed utterly. The way that cop smashed my guitar.

Eye-to-eye Vanbrugh and I regarded each other, and *he* was the only man I couldn't match. My gaze swerved and muddied, confronted with his. I failed. I loved him. Melva's sixteen-year-old boy, Curly, had a pill-fevered glassy slack-jawed control that almost threw me—like staring into the eyes of a corpse—but I managed to burn him down, the little bastard. And at the Stauntons' campaign party for Senator Rutland up in Wildrose Canyon I confronted a rival who tried to woo Melva from my side, a platinum-haired boy with twitchy jaw muscles but steelish eyes I somehow thought I had confronted before, maybe Inside, or maybe at one of the psychiatric units I did time in, and for several tense moments it looked as if the little bastard might win. . . . But he didn't. He lost. He faltered and dipped and broke and was ground down to nothing by Gotteson's will.

When I die, it will be by a shutting-off of my energy valves *from within.* I will decompose while they stare at me, trying to pump life back into me so that I can be returned to Death Row, and what a commotion it will be, rushing me into the emergency ward to get my heart started again before my brain pops too many cells, what noise, what fury, what a clanging of bells and screaming of sirens! But since my energies arise entirely from my soul they are controlled from within; and no technological wonders from the Outside are going to juice me up again. Let the District Attorney (wired to react with rage) protest all he wishes, and even threaten to bring malpractice charges against the physicians who labored to save me but of course failed!—for though Gotteson slipped up a little in being born, he will not err in his dying. All death is of course suicide. So we have Gotteson in his triumph. . . .

The Assumption of the Spider Monkey.

14

Soul-Programming

Danny Minx sometimes known as Danny Blecher sometimes known as *The Eye* taught me to program my soul; but
joked so much, tickled me so much, that the lessons never
exactly sank in. Not until I was alone in California, hitch-hiking
up and down the coast, sleeping on the shell-hardened sand,
edging up to drive-in restaurants to see what I could find in
trash-cans or to beg little short-skirted waitresses for hand-outs,
and not really until I made my way along the Strip seeking a
job, did the conscious utilization of Soul-Programming tech-
niques come to fruition. Those big beautiful billboards on
Sunset Boulevard helped me. I don't know exactly how. Helped
me tune into something, latch onto something, the way my
guitar strummed on its own . . . receiving words for me as if
words came from outer space to me alone, because I was
worthy of receiving them. I could set my soul-program for
Introspective-Shy or *-Volatile.* The entire world was open to be
imagined in those days. *Genius, Gentle.* Or *Genius, Mad.* But
the summer of my ascendancy, the four-nights-a-week gig at
Lucky Pierre's, I set myself to a style indefinable though some
might call it *Sloe-Eyed Gypsy, American.*

When Melva and her friends met me, though, they pinched
and nuzzled and tongue-tickled me for *The Outlaw, The Devil,
Sheik,* and other corny old-lady ideas maybe taken from the
movies or TV, and it was just to shock them and maybe disgust
them (Melva and her lady friends like being disgusted) that I
told them I was in essence a Spider Monkey, in my soul, with a
looping furry cunning tail scrunched up inside my trousers.
Melva shrieked with laughter and said, Jesus, her boys had been
right about me, they'd picked a winner this time—those devils!
She was very fond of me. She was fond of me from the first. I

57

completed her trio of boys, shorter by some inches than the kids themselves, and the four of us could go anywhere, publicly observed and unsuspicious, Melva herding us into dairy restaurants and into coffee shops and into Venice Park funhouses, tanned and glaring-beautiful in her leggy billowing pants, all of us set for *Family Fun.*

But I was her chauffeur at the movie premiere where we chatted with Richard S., the talent scout who handled Fritzie D. B., that mascara-dripping mush-mouthed little singer whose fifty-foot face I had to stare at, across from Lucky Pierre's all summer long: how I envied Fritzie D. B.! Like me he was over thirty but like me he looked about nineteen. But droopy-eyed, mushy-mouthed! The bastard! And with Richard S. in one corner of the gay-lit theater lobby I deftly switched to *Substitute for Fritzie . . . ?* And it was uncanny, how Richard S. got that message. He really got it. He stared at me, blinking, while Melva chattered away, and even took out his eyeglasses and put them on, to stare at me all the more, while I gazed eye-to-eye with him sending message after message, *all of which he received.* I know it. But Fritzie D. B. is still living, still alive, still recording his songs and collecting gold records, a millionaire at the age of thirty-one; it was his agent who died, found dead of an overdose of something, at his boat-house in Malibu. By then it was too late for me anyway, I'd dropped out of that world, by then . . . I think, yes, by then I had already slipped into my destiny. . . .

I had programmed for *Revenger.* And *Hero-of-Headlines.* And even *Sex Maniac.* And: *Spider Monkey Triumphs.*

15

Above the Sea

—fifteen hundred feet. The air was wet. The sun came out a few times while we were there but in other parts of the sky everything was wet and heavy. Fog moved in like a wall but somewhere else, where I didn't think there was a horizon, the sun was setting. The reflections of the sun jumped back and forth and made me dizzy.

I said to them, I hate this place. I hate the wind up here. So I stayed for a while in the front seat of the Rolls-Royce, where I had sometimes slept anyway, just to be alone and away from their noise and their grinning. Melva came out to me, walking barefoot on the sharp-edged gravel, wincing and whimpering to get my attention. "Bobbie, there's a rainbow. The sky is filled with a rainbow. Bobbie, don't you care?" she said. I lay with my head down on the seat, not sleeping or trying to sleep, only blank, blanked-out. While she tapped at the window it began to rain again. She had a whining singsong voice not meant for me to hear: ". . . engagement or adoption? . . . Engagement or adoption?"

Some of them said, Go on and get engaged to him!—marry him!

Others said, Adopt him!

One of her sons wanted me as a brother. He thought it would be fun. The other son, the zonked-out one, the one I sometimes feared, wanted me as a *father*. He tugged at Melva's bracelets and whispered so that I could hear, "I want a father. I already got one brother and I hate him. Now I want a father. I don't remember my father. I want a new father—I want Bobbie as a father. I want him. I want *him*." Glassy-eyed, droop-mouthed, he grinned at me and seemed to be seeing things in the air between himself and me.

The little bastard. He'll be the first to go, I thought.

16

Hitting Off

Some of them were shooting at the hawks. Paddy and
Colette and June and a girl named Irma, who went a little crazy,
imitating the birds in their wide-winged evil circling, in a dance
she made up as she danced on the flagstone "landing terrace."
Melva was very jealous of her. Vlad J. following us all over
with his hand-held camera, one of Melva's boys climbing down
through the rubble to the beach, slipping and cutting his bare
leg on a rock, blood swarming out. I laughed and climbed down
to rescue him—this was the second day and I was still powerful
—and tested out his blood myself, dipping a forefinger in it just
for wild laughter, and the kid went white.

At night you could hear rattlesnakes. You could hear
slithering and cold evil crawling. The inside of the place was so
jumbled, so smelling of wet people and their things, that I
went back out to sleep in the car. I like to sleep alone. Out there
my head was filled with the pounding of water, pounding
pounding pulsing of great waves, water breaking against the
beach against the boulders. The boulders were big as houses. I
cast my mind back over the partying and the filming and
wondered: Was Gotteson like that foam down there, churning
out of the Pacific Ocean only to be sucked back into
nothing . . . ?

Vlad J. said he couldn't see except through his camera.
Couldn't see things in three-dimensional focus. His eyes
fastened on mine, through the camera lens. He said, Bobbie you
have the most fascinating face, Bobbie, your face is . . . your
face is fascinating. . . . Your body is fascinating. . . . You
climbed up here, didn't you, climbed up from the beach or out
of a hole in the ground, with little bits of dirt clinging to you,
clinging to the hairs on your body, your fingers itching to get at
us . . . ?

I did the Machete Dance for him. Irma ran out to join me, eyes closed and stomach bared. *Do it, do it!* she begged. The others took up the chant. But though I was high from hitting off the blood a sweat broke over me and I went cold. Irma screamed: *Do it to me, Bobbie!* Floating in the pool and cast in a heap at the end of the pool were the mannequins from yesterday. Irma was like foam being churned up and flung at me, her mouth twisted, saliva running from one corner of her mouth down her chin, the others were gathered around chanting and stamping their feet, sweet Bobbie and sweet Irma, why not . . . ?

Why not?

Somebody said that the scavenger birds could see death, could see life about to *click!* into death. That was why they circled El Portal all the time. Their shrewd lidless eyes were like mine. Could pierce surfaces that are a riddle to ordinary vision. There, there—there the fizzing-out of life, and *there* Bobbie swoops down to his target! Irma rushed at me. There were black smears around her eyes, her eyeballs were watering, itching, reddened. She was going to die anyway in a few weeks. The sea and sky and these chanting hoarse people were too much for her . . . she was someone's ex-daughter or ex-wife . . . she was "under contract" at V. Studios and hadn't had a job for six years, assigned to wait, she had wept into my ear the night before of how she had been a Queen somewhere—Davenport?—Davenport High School?—a *Queen*—and her beautiful face and beautiful black mane of hair had won her so many prizes and loves and this contract under Mr. V. but now she was a very old woman, ready to die, she was twenty-two years old and please, Bobbie, would I kill her so that she could break back into tiny particles of moisture, . . . ? She threw her arms around my neck but I swung the Machete clear of her with a trick I had, so that people gasped, and if I had not been so steady in my center of gravity she would have knocked us both into the pool.

At this moment the sun broke clear. Vlad J. ran up to us. "Oh, the sun! The sun!"

We rubbed our eyes and put on dark glasses.

Everyone denies these accusations, Bobbie. You are telling lies.

61

He came down himself. He came to visit. *He* came to visit. El Portal is in his name, you can check it—

El Portal is not in his name.

He came himself to visit, there are pictures of him! They all got out their cameras. Vlad J. filmed the landing of the helicopters. I was there. Someone ran to wake me up, I was lying in the main living room, with my head in the fireplace where the stone was very cold and restful, and I ran outside in spite of how burning the sun was, and there the first helicopter was landing. . . . I went wild with it, the roaring and whining! I was very excited! Everyone had been arguing—would he show up, or wouldn't he?—even though it was Melva's birthday and some anniversary of theirs—but one of Melva's boys had confided in me that *he* had forgotten all about Melva, that *he* was in love with someone else and would never show up at this dump. . . . But he was supposed to come to meet me. This was to be our meeting.

You really are a maniac, Bobbie. It's pathetic, actually. That you, a no-talent two-bit three-time-loser punk from New Jersey, a State-supported little ungrateful bastard with fake gypsy eyes and a voice like coffee grounds—that you of all people should fantasize a meeting with the millionaire-industrialist, millionaire-inventor, millionaire-philanthropist Vanbrugh!

The first helicopter landed on the terrace. Some men climbed out and circled the terrace. I was a little off my head from the roaring because I hate machines. *I'm* no mechanical modern man! They were dressed in suits and ties and knew their way around, Melva invited them inside for a drink, but they said no, they didn't have time, but had to clean things up a little for Mr. V. who would be landing in an hour, and everyone looked at everyone else—scruffy and red-eyed and wild-haired from the night before—and Irma started to cry and staggered back to the house. I smoothed my hair down with my hands. They got the Mexican servants to clean up and one of Mr. V.'s aides and myself dragged junk out of the swimming pool, he was very polite to me, and appreciated it when I said I'd wade in, to get some bottles and parts of dummies' arms and legs that were floating around, so he wouldn't have to get his shirt-cuff wet. Then they sprayed. They explained that Mr. V. was very cautious about scorpions. I followed them around and helped move chairs and tables and beach-umbrellas. I said that I had a magic way with poisonous things, that I could pick up a scorpion up and talk it out of stinging. It was a matter of inner rhythms. It was a matter of slowing your brain-rhythms to such an extent that the scorpion swayed with you, hypnotized. They were very polite to me and—

Bobbie, all this is a lie. You know that you never met any of these people. They deny it. Most of them deny it. And if you weren't under indictment for first-degree murder, for having hacked to death one Cynthia Pryce of Pasadena, California, you can be certain that the Vanbrugh Corporation would sue you for all you possess—

I did meet him. I met all of them. It's on film but I can't get hold of the film and I can't get royalties from it. The girl from Pasadena has nothing to do with it. I don't know her. I met her in a bar. She followed me out. She was a stewardess for TransContinental Airlines and in my head I got it mixed up with *his* airlines—I hate machines and can't remember their names—something lurched up in me, like a log lurching up to the surface of some fast-moving wild stream, and I thought, Hey why not, hey, why not go home with this little doll and love her a little, and maybe, maybe she is a little girl of *his* to put in another good word for you, Bobbie? . . . because by then I was broke and desperate and everyone had slammed the door shut in Bobbie's face. Because I was sinking and bruised. I didn't know her name and in the bungalow, in the front room where she showed me all her girl friends' record albums, and we were fooling around, a mist came over my brain the way it floated over the railing from the sea. I got sick. Very sick. Throwing-up-sick. And so certain powers failed me and no soul-programming worked, and the girl started to throw herself around like she was crazy, and I was throwing myself around like there were many more of me, inside of me, crammed-up inside of me . . . like a woman stuffed with babies, baby rats or baby gophers or moles or . . . or things burrowing to get out, you know, and ready to use their teeth if they can't get out. When I came to the lights in the front room were smashed and the hi-fi was blaring, drums and rockets coming from two sides of the room, and I crawled over the broken records and the cushions with their stuffing hacked out and I saw this dressmaker's dummy with one shoe on and one shoe off and a lot of blood, and a weird red glow from the hi-fi where there was this little pink-scarlet knob, you know, made of plastic, that lit up to tell you that there was still electric current going there. . . . My mind opened up a crack and alerted me to rise on one elbow, to look around for the camera. Was maybe somebody lurking in the kitchen, in the dark? . . . eh? . . . was it little owl-eyed Vlad J. who loved me so, and all but thrust Irma into my nest in the fireplace? . . . or someone from the studio itself, The Studio, getting a few hundred yards more of film for them to scrutinize? But I didn't have my guitar any longer! I did have the Machete with me, which I usually carried wound in many yards of coarse woven cloth some girl gave me, brought back from Taos, to go with my primitive good looks, but where was the Machete . . . ?

The dressmaker's dummy with all the blood was lying on it. The handle was showing. Weird-red, glowing-red, pink-scarlet-sinister radiance. It glowed in the dark. I crawled over to her and said, "Honey, you didn't tell me your name, even," and it wasn't until later that day when I had escaped and was having a tamale-burger at a Strip drive-in, standing near some teenage bastard and his bright yellow Ferrari with the radio blaring, that I heard the news bulletin, but by then . . . by then the memory of it had all evaporated and I felt only that fuzzy little interest, you know, that you feel when you hear about four or five stewardesses murdered in some bungalow they rented out in Pasadena that the neighbors swore had been raided three times in the last three months, for drugs and wild parties and late-night-noises, so I had only a foggy good citizen's interest in that, because my real self was with my music but my music was shut off and all those powers that went with it, that I lost in the scramble-climb up Vanbrugh's house while those bastards stood around clapping and cheering and snickering—

Bobbie, you're lying. You were never at Vanbrugh's house: that house outside Lucia is not owned by him. Not according to the county's records. You didn't meet Vanbrugh, not Vanbrugh in person. You met an aide of his. It was a joke. It was a costume-party. It was a Mardi Gras party. It was a joke set up by Dewey L. of The Studio to punish Melva for her loudmouth talk about him having to sell his house and move into a four-bedroom Colonial in the Junior Estates sub-division off Mulholland Drive, because he was being blackmailed through some convoluted contacts culminating in a dead drug-pusher's close friend up at Berkeley who possesses certain embarrassing photos involving the dead boy and Mr. L.'s daughter. . . . So it was all a trick, Bobbie, to fool everyone at El Portal, just some actors dressed up as Mr. V.'s flying squad and that degenerate decrepit character-actor of the Forties, Edwin E. playing Vanbrugh himself. What a joke! What a complicated maze!

I looked him in the eyes. Eye-to-eye with him. I *saw* him. I *saw*. They had to help him down the ladder, he must have been unwell. He walked tilted a little to one side . . . his right shoulder was higher than his left shoulder. . . . He wore a gauze mask that hid all of his face except the eyes. One of the aides helped him . . . and he walked over to a table they'd set up for him, the Mexicans all dressed now in white, the blood- and gut-smeared outfits of yesterday gone and clean starched white outfits on, white-gloved, and even the slow-cruising buzzards seemed to stare down at him. I felt my center of gravity tilt. . . . I felt a strange tugging in my brain, where so much had been hoarded up, so much sanity and the need to run to someone and seize his ankle and howl like a wolf, to surrender oh sweet Jesus at last . . . after so many years . . . to surrender instead of having them all surrender to me, turning themselves inside-out to me and their shallow little dark crevices wet-aching for me, *for me,* the way a few weeks later all their moist little pores would be crying out for me to open them, but when *he* came to me, when the second helicopter landed and the hurricane-whirling subsided and his nicest politest young aide in a blue suit and a dark blue necktie and a white shirt led him over to the table, even though he was an older man as I could see, and walked unsteadily, and his gray-black hair was thinning so that an oval of his scalp showed through, *so very ordinary* that the terrace and the helicopters and the broken-up towers of fog coming to us from the ocean were changed into something else, the cries of the birds changed, everything shrill and breathless and burning with sun, and where oh God was my guitar?—where had I left it?—when this happened I knew I would never be the same again. I stood there hypnotized. He sat down, he looked at us. One of the servants uncorked a bottle of water and another servant uncorked a bottle of California wine and, while he watched carefully and indicated with a deft movement of his forefinger—he wore dark gloves—how high they should pour the mixture in a goblet, I seemed to hear the thought-message shooting around into all of us: *Stay where you are until you're released!*

17

Gotteson's Pilot-Film

They came into motion again.

It began to pulse with time and waves again, and little tentative giggles from the girls. And sound began again. And he motioned Melva over and for forty-five minutes she crouched beside him, not daring to sit, and the two of them talked together in whispers and I saw her face change and age and wither and turn greenish-metallic and brighten again and turn into the face of a twenty-five-year-old girl smiling glowing up into the gauzed-over face of a gentleman who had descended to her from the sky and would soon ascend again but in the meantime was almost touching her, almost touching her tear-sparkling cheeks, while the aides moved among us and said cheerfully, Don't just stand around looking so scared!—let's have some nice music piped out here or maybe some of you could entertain—*he* doesn't like anything fussy or fancy, just tap-dancing or even ballroom dancing if there's enough room—his tastes are very simple! We were all shy until Paddy cleared his throat and said, Hey Jesus, this sure takes me back, and he sucked in air for two-three-four laborious seconds and licked his lips and fastened his blood-cobwebbed gaze on a point just a few inches to the left of Mr. V.'s table and began a little dance-routine that I had never seen before in anyone. He lost his balance and started over. Someone said, You've still got it, Paddy! And someone else, a middle-aged tear-brimming blond who had nibbled my toes the night before, snatched off her shoes and began to match Paddy in his dance, spreading out her arms and fixing a sweet glassy smile on the distance, and the two of them danced carefully, grinning, at first pretending not to be aware of each other and then coming together face-to-face with a foot or more between them, while Colette hummed very loudly and broke into a song that the others joined—

A one, a two, a dippety-dippety-do—

And where was my guitar?

Vlad J. slid his arm around my neck and said softly, "Honey, let's swing right into a proposition we've all been meaning to make you, and now is the perfect time, let's explore the possibilities of a comedy series in which you play the role . . . a timely role, and I have the go-ahead from a very interested producer at The Studio, unfortunately not with us right now, but a quick telephone call would get him out here fast if he *knew* . . . who happened to be here. Anyway it is a most timely role and Melva balked because she has this mania for troubadours, I mean the funky gutsy strong stuff, but I'm going to go over Melva's head and take the chance and put the proposition to you, man, because I know you don't have an agent, don't believe in agents, but look here, honey, the idea some of us cooked up together was: a comedy series with you as the star's side-kick, the one who gets all the laughs or most of them, the one who sort of steals the scenes, you know, up until the last five minutes when things straighten out and the drama gets prepared for The End, but anyway you've got this incredible natural fantastic talent for being so goddam funny . . . I mean aside from your other talents . . . but this is going to be a family show, you know, on television. On television. And some of us thought, Jesus, it was almost a spontaneous group-thought, that I should do maybe a pilot-film while we're all together out here, like a family, pretty well-acquainted by now and not so self-conscious, and now with Mr. Vanbrugh among us, what an ideal opportunity!—I make enough in six weeks to finance me the rest of the year, so I can do the kind of film-making I really want . . . and the kind that is somehow in my nature . . . *my unique inexplicable nature demanding to be given visual form* . . . And so honey, my proposition to you is—"

I pushed him away.

I turned and ran back toward the house.

I was already crying, hoarse angry sobs, and behind me

they stopped singing and dancing and said, "What . . . ?
What's wrong . . . ? What happened . . . ?"

I ran through the foyer and slid on the white fur rugs and
almost fell, my eyes were blurred with tears, and righted my
balance and ran through the big sunken living room and along
the hallway past the Spanish tapestries and icons and in my rage
I knocked a statue off its pedestal, and ran into one of the back
bedrooms and tore at the bedspread, a heavy primitive quilt
with cougars and American eagles and fir trees woven into it,
and threw the pillows around tearing one of the pillows with
my teeth so that fine white fluffy pinfeathers swirled everywhere, and I heard someone calling after me, *Oh Bobbie!* and
my mind blanked out and I tried to crawl under the bed,
because I remember lying under there with my eyes shut tight to
keep the tears back and dust-balls drawn up to my mouth when
I breathed in and pushed a few inches back when I breathed out,
and Melva herself was kneeling by the bed and saying, "Oh
Bobbie, did he hurt your feelings . . . ? Oh Bobbie! Oh Jesus, I
told him to let me talk to you. He's a Russian, he's never learned
the nuances of our language . . . don't pay any attention to
him, Bobbie, please come back out . . . please don't cry . . .
Mr. Vanbrugh saw you run away and he's *very*, very upset, he
can't stand for anyone to be sad in his presence, he's a
wonderful and generous man and so seldom meets interesting
people like us, he's usually surrounded with that squad of
Harvard Law bastards that you can't get through to save your
soul. . . . Bobbie, sweetheart, are you listening? Mr. Vanbrugh
himself wants to see you perform. *Mr. Vanbrugh himself.* He's
asking for you, he's out there actually requesting that you come
back . . . he was angry with Vlad for upsetting you, and Vlad
may just be out of a job if one of Mr. V.'s aides takes a dislike to
him, but you could make us all so happy . . . and yourself so
happy! . . . if you'd just come back out, honey, and show us
how funny you are. There's no story-line cooked up yet, for the
comedy series, and they don't have a male lead but it will be not
trouble to find one—some tall blond clean-faced boring kid,
maybe a surfer, or a singer with a good voice—and *you*,
Bobbie, would be the scene-stealer! Did Vlad tell you all this?
Honey, please come back! Please forgive Vlad, in front of Mr.
V., so he won't get in trouble! We're all like a big family, even

those of us who don't know one another well, it's all one party, honey, and please don't be uppity. . . . Mr. V. had the idea that you were one of my sons, he seems to think you're a bit younger than you are. . . . So come back, honey, let me wipe your face . . . that's my good sweet Bobbie, yes . . . yes, crawl back out here. . . . You've been crying and your face is all dirty. Let me just wipe it clean, honey, so Mr. V. can see how striking a face you have. . . . Such personality! Such bone-structure!"

18

Louise D.'s Birthday/Deathday

Telepathic nudges and winks drew me to her.

I can alter my own blood chemistry to release Truth Serum into my veins, in order not to lie, because I despise liars and would not stand among them. I don't lie. It was telepathic beams that drew me over there, and no old grudges against her. I didn't know her. I had only met her through a pal, who'd been her patient at some hospital or other, and he introduced us one morning at somebody's house-party, and kept saying, "Louise, you'd *love* Bobbie! You could *never* psych out our Bobbie!" She was taller than me, which I didn't like, and too loud and robust and joking, in her thirties, high on something or other and sounding off about some bastards in the legislature who were trying to cut back on mental health funds, which might mean she'd be out of her job, whatever it was, and she kept swaying and putting her hands on me, but I had my eye that morning on a skinny-legged small-faced blonde with mournful smudged eyes who was barefoot and lonely and needed taking in hand for a weekend, maybe, and so I didn't pay Louise D. much mind, because I had enough of big energetic cheerful-weepy women with Melva and her friends though somehow I liked Louise D. and had the idea, well maybe, maybe if she was my sister or something, she'd help me out, talking confidentially and quietly the way that lady therapist had talked to me out in Nevada: I had appreciated her interest in making me well. But it was crowded in the house and the skinny blonde was also eying me, sending little terrified dart-messages of *Help me, love me, take me in hand*, so Bobbie excused himself and headed for the little girl. And he didn't regret it either because she turned out to be Baby Sharleen and an important contact.

But Louise's liquid-bright eager eyes sank into my soul, so

that I dreamt them out clear one night when I didn't even think I had been sleeping, when I'd already lost the guitar and was lying under some bushes in a park with my book-bag under my head stuffed with my personal possessions and the Machete, of course, inside its yards of special Indian cloth. This was three or four or maybe five days after the Pasadena bungalow and the girls who turned out not to be stewardesses for the right airline, but all that was foggy and insignificant.

I saw Louise D.'s eyes turning onto me. Focussing. I sat up and rubbed my face.

At first I did not recognize the eyes. I let them focus inside me. I didn't prod myself, didn't ask questions. A spark of excitement began, but I paid it no mind. I was done with loving. (". . . farewell to love / loving . . .") The love-power would not last me, not since I toppled off that tower or turret or whatever people called it at El Portal, clamber-climbing up the vines that turned out to be bug-eaten, while the audience cheered clapped urged me on, consumer-bastards—and so I set my mind fiercely away from that part of my body. Though nobody believes me I must repeat for the record: I never valued such behavior.

Muffled outraged incredulous laughter in the courtroom.

I didn't! I didn't value it! . . . Everyone else did, the girls and the women and the spectators here in Court and the slobbering old-young men, even Danny, even my master Danny, but *I never did* because it was monkey-antics, monkey-tricks, black-spidery-monkey grappling and wrestling to earn a few bucks, however you lyricize it. Except for the immediate loss of my contacts—how they all deserted me, the pricks!—I didn't mind the fall and the shock to my vertebrae and my glands and the part of my brain that secretes the power-juices, I didn't even mind all of them laughing . . . though sometimes that raucous laughter returns to me here in my cell or in Court. . . . *I didn't mind* that crucifixion because Mr. V. alone did not laugh, though it could be argued that he engineered everything. No, for the record it must be said that I did not mind anything that happened to The Spider Monkey. But my music, my powers of music!—my soul!

Did you have the idea, Bobbie, that Louise D. would help you?

Yes. No. I don't know. I thought . . . I thought maybe . . . maybe a big girl like that, a big-sister, maybe she'd . . . she would sit and make me tea or something and I could explain to her about the guitar that was smashed, and how my contacts were all out of town when I called them, and how Melva had flown to Majorca with her boys and someone else whose identity I couldn't learn, because people were lying to me right and left! . . . and I could explain about the stewardesses and how the amplified sound had given me powers I didn't exactly want, beamed in to me from some rock-group's soul, and how the Machete had acted of its own volition, hacking away and saying, "Who's your cute little monkey boy-friend now, honey, *who's* your portable plug-in dark smouldering rent-a-monkey now?" while she kicked and tried to crawl out the front door. . . . And it was a fiasco! A mess! And I thought that Louise whoever-she-was would understand all this, because she'd made such an impression on my pal that he talked her up often, and showed up at her apartment one night with a cop's helmet he'd gotten off a cop, him and some other boys, and kidded around with her saying, *Hey Louise!—we killed a cop tonight! —we killed a pig tonight, want to celebrate?—* And evidently she hadn't acted too alarmed, but asked the boys to please go away, she was so sleepy and the neighbors would be listening, they were nosey, please go away boys and no rough-house, you don't want to get into trouble. . . . So I thought I would run to her.

And did she let you in?

Oh yes! She opened the door and recognized me, she was like a nurse, a mother, a teacher, a big-breasted lady older than me and wiser, standing there in a green flannel bathrobe with something white and flaky on her face. . . . She recognized me right away. She said *Oh! come in, you're Jerry's friend the singer, what's wrong with you?—why are you looking so blue? Are you still playing at Lucky Pierre's? Are you alone?*

She poured us both a drink though I don't drink and breathed rapidly and noisily at me, her pudgy shoulders hunched forward, not to miss a word, and I told her weeping about the days I had to hide because I was so sick-looking and

73

the scavenging I did in garbage bins out back of the drive-in restaurants and the supermarkets, pawing through the spoiled meat to get to the fruit and vegetables because I didn't want to hit off raw flesh without others around to move in rhythm with me, and she seemed to understand, and her eyes filled with tears when I described crawling into a Salvation Army pick-up bin (though this had taken place a decade ago, in Newark) to get a few clothes, and almost falling helplessly inside, and the terror I felt then, and my mind leaped around the kitchen where we were sitting and I had the sudden idea that *this kitchen was familiar to me* and that the words I uttered here would be taped, recorded, somehow preserved in someone's memory who was not exactly here in the room with us, but maybe connected with this Louise D. who worked for some mental research clinic and could not be trusted. . . . My mind skittered onto one of my mothers, and onto another of them, and focussed again on Louise D. who was staring at me with a small strange smile that showed just part of one of her big milky oversized front teeth, and I heard her saying, "Bobbie, don't be afraid now, Bobbie, Bobbie why don't you just . . . just sit still. . . . I have this friend, this doctor-friend, I would like to call, who can administer something to you to, you know, help you sleep if you'd like to sleep, on my sofa maybe, you're certainly welcome to sleep on my sofa . . . I'd love to have you rest up here. . . . So if you'd just relax and sip some of that drink, or maybe you'd like some milk . . . I could warm up some milk . . . some chocolate milk. . . . And then we could talk about this more quietly . . . and then . . . and. . . ."

But I interrupted all this. I tried to explain to her about the pilot-film, and how I had been doing so well standing on my hands and leaping about and when I began my climb, my monkey-climb, up the side of the house I had the audience with me all the way, breath-by-breath, and if she moved off that kitchen chair I'd slit her throat, and I didn't need any doctor-friend to put me to sleep, no thank you, though maybe I'd take her up on that offer of a nap on her sofa because I was *very tired.* She was about to jump up from the chair to help me, and I grinned at her one of my old slash-grins that must have been a genetic compulsion, a programmed characteristic, since I had never known anyone Inside or Out who could smile the way I did; so she sat back down again. She wasn't very pretty. I don't know why I had thought she was pretty. Her skin was yellowish the way Melva's was at times, early in the morning when her make-up was soured and filmed-over with perspiration, the way my tongue tasted at this moment, scummy and not well. *All I wanted, Louise, was to be a face on a billboard!—was that too much to ask?*

Poem for Louise

The Olympic swimmer swimming to triumph
The sparrow-hawk diving to triumph
Gotteson weeping in dustballs beneath a bed
or kissing hairs loose on a rug
or warm and curly with life
or sticky-drying on the Machete blade—

you did not look like the bastard
who gave me a hypodermic in Reno
or like "Louise D." on the front page
beneath the headline FIFTH MURDER
but like Gotteson craving crawling on the Strip
and like the Olympic high-jumper jumping
like Christ on the pole of All Knowing
we live right up to the last second
in one big triumph

I spoke to her evenly and quickly. I knew there was not much time. I told her that Gotteson without his guitar was deadly, that to brush against me would be like brushing against a scorpion, so charged-up, so coiled-back, and that my trouble had always been people crowding too close, causing static to interfere with my natural powers, falling under my spell and begging me for love, even for intimate little husbandly chores like plucking some woman's eyebrows for her in a steamy bathroom with music piped in. . . . I told her about the clinic someone had dragged me to, back in Newark, where I had to sit on a bench for an hour and a half, and where I wet my pants, and the other kids began to giggle, one of them a six-foot moron wagging his finger at me. The air in that stuffy steam-heated place had burst into pieces of knife-blades, flying everywhere, and not even little Bobbie himself could escape their wrath! *Louise, sit still. Louise, don't move.* She began to cry. She said that yesterday had been her birthday. I asked her, how old? and she shook her head slowly as if pretending she had not heard, and I said, honey, you don't look more than thirty to me, and she didn't take me up on the compliment but just kept staring at my hands, which I had to hold still to keep from moving hypnotically, a corny habit of mine I must have got from one of my show-business friends. I said, I bet she was very kind to her patients, she had that kind cheerful big-sister look that meant so much to sick people, especially men. But the sparks-out-of-my-brain were a little too much for both of us, I think she could feel them, she began to tremble and just sat there staring at my hands, and I tried to keep my voice down because of the neighbors (somehow I knew about the neighbors being nosey) to explain that I was still that child on the bench in Newark, still innocent though fouling my pants and still being laughed at, though now that I was an adult I could strike back at those who laughed. She whispered that yesterday had been her birthday . . . and I said to her, now yesterday is over . . . it's three-thirty in the morning and a new day for you . . . and you didn't want another birthday rolling around anyway, did you?

In that kitchen both of us learned that God is a Maniac like me: out-guessing and out-hyping me. My wildest soaring song came to me in a rush-of-words like a spasm *Hate hate hate hate hate hate hate pity.* You start with *Hate* and end with *Pity.* So I hacked her free of being Female, caught there inside a big bulk of raw flesh, scented with Lilac Talcum Powder from the corner drugstore, the two of us grappling and sliding around on the slippery linoleum, Gotteson knowing deep in his brain the truth of the words of a small cartoon-vision of Gotteson, instructing him that he *talked too goddam much, and now look!* Yet I was out-guessed by the God of the Night, Gotteson himself out-done by the energies that came to him, and crept away exhausted and self-disgusted before four AM, with no one the wiser. If the neighbors heard anything they didn't let on.

Defense Counsel requests that it be stricken from the record that the Accused made any reference to "God." The Accused, that is, the Maniac, protests that at that time in his life he did believe, he seemed to have sudden knowledge of, the truth of God's Mania for Man, His Mania for All of Man (and not just Part), and God's being able to easily outstrip Man in Fantastic Imagination and Deeds. He meant to honor God! He certainly meant to honor God, as one Maniac honors another! —But the courtroom is noisy, the Judge is actually banging his gavel, the television cameramen don't know which face to zoom up to, the Maniac sits stricken and impotent in his sweat-drenched thirty-dollar suit, so baggy on his emaciated body and so different from the cruisewear he used to own only a few months ago. He cannot even remember a woman named "Louise D." and though he is not on trial for her murder (one woman at a time!) he is very sorry to have forgotten her. He remembers a green bathrobe. He remembers a slightly protruding front tooth.

And so, Bobbie, in your activities as a killer you followed the same basic pattern of promiscuity begun so many years ago, as a boy in Juvenile Detention . . . ? Through you, or boys just like you, diseases are spread across the continent. There is an epidemic of diseases, isn't there? What we are asking you, Bobbie, is just this: to the best of your knowledge is it possible that you are only a pawn?—a tool?—that you and diseased boys like you are actually being used by intelligent forces to infect the American continent with debilitating and brain-rotting diseases . . . ?

No.

But it is a possibility, isn't it? We find it remarkable that someone as degenerate as yourself, as mentally deficient as our records show you to be and your dull-eyed appearance argues you actually are, can answer that question so confidently!

Throughout my life I did worry about that—about influences. About the way the moon acted upon the ocean, and how it might act upon me. After the stormy session in Louise's kitchen, when I must have blacked out for ten, oh maybe fifteen minutes, and just seemed to fall through the floor and keep on falling, and threshing around, arms and legs, hacking and plunging and gasping for breath, oh sweet Jesus I had to take stock of myself. I was frightened. I begged for some change by the Brown Derby, where the doorman seemed to recognize me and asked how Melva was, and I lied to him and said she was spending a few weeks at a beauty farm north of San Diego, and hoped he wouldn't notice my unconvincing tone of voice or the nail-scratches on my face, and excused myself as soon as I had collected a few dollars' worth of change, and went to a flophouse downtown to take a shower and shave and I turned the water on Cold to give myself a shock; to make myself think. I had to think: *Which direction was I headed in?* It had always upset me, to witness the strange powers of the moon, the rising and sinking-back of the tide, and to apply that to my own life, to think that maybe someone or *something* was influencing me without my knowledge. I had always received my music, gratefully. I had "received" it without question. But these recent events, the Machete leaping into such life, sweeping and plunging and pulsating and throbbing in a way the guitar had not, this frightened me because my soul blacked out at such times and abandoned me to whatever was going on. So I stood there under the cold freezing shower and thought of penance. Doing penance. Getting my mind straight and reason-driven, Bobbie Gotteson in his own head again, not running wild. I had a terrible vision of one of the chickens out at El Portal, running with its neck cut and blood flying everywhere, and how the girls screamed, and jerked their legs back so the blood wouldn't get on them, and I seemed to feel myself inside that chicken, running and squawking helplessly, and I thought of how one of my buddies at Terminal Island had explained to me how a kindly teacher of his once taught him to conquer his stammering: *by making himself stammer on purpose.*

19

Doreen B.

A penitential act. A Negative Act. An Undoing-of-Magic Act.

Why, I didn't even know her! Therefore, no personal motives. No personal revenge. She reminded me somewhat of Irma, though shorter and plainer than Irma, just a secretary or typist-appearing girl, that I followed home from the beach and saw how lonely she was, her heels worn down, and her bleached hair wilted from the humidity that day. I followed her right up to her apartment on the third floor of a walk-up, but she closed the door on me and for some reason I didn't want to knock, I thought she might stare at me through the peep-hole, and, somehow, *recognize me*, so I waited until dark and climbed up the side of her building, hand-over-hand, concentrating on not falling, on one brick after another, very slowly, cautiously, though there was no moonlight to guide me or to illuminate the blade of the Machete, as I pretended there was in my poem. In fact, the Machete was wrapped in its carrying-cloth and stuck in my book-bag, which had a strap so that I could carry it over my shoulder—

The District Attorney throws down his wad of notes, pretending to be at his wits' end and now embarked on spontaneous impromptu cross-examination, and even the front-row spectators look frightened and guilty, he is so angry, and he shouts in a terrible voice that echoes high in the ceiling of this 19th-century building, where airplane-propeller-sized fans rotate to stir the humid air: "Gotteson, just where did you come from? Just who are you?" (Someone at the back of the courtroom yells: "Out of the locker, you know where he came from!" and we all turn to see who it is, but the police have already ushered

the girl out—she must be one of the "Liberate All Prisoners"
pickets who are hanging around outside, complete strangers to
me, and from what I have gathered the same rich kids who
made my life miserable when I was begging for small change,
seriously and desperately, while they were having fun putting
their hands out to tourists—oh, what I could do to them all,
what I'd surely do if I were liberated!)

In my cell I have thought about this. I "think" all the time,
even when I am asleep. Or maybe it should be put differently—
thoughts come to me, thoughts "think" me. Sometimes I am
wrenched with spasms of thought-waves, running through me
the way, in the old days, convulsions used to go through those I
loved with my finest most meticulous style, during which time
there was no "Bobbie Gotteson" any more than there was any
human being there, the object of my love-power. On the
Outside, concerned so much with my career and caught up in a
frenzied rapid-living crowd of middle-aged people, mainly,
except for the young girls whose sunken eyes were so middle-
aged, I did not have time to notice all this. I thought that *Bobbie*
Gotteson was doing the thinking. Now, I know better. Now, I
know that *thoughts* are thinking Bobbie Gotteson; Bobbie
Gotteson *is* a thought-spasm. Sometimes he is more than a
thought, and sometimes a spasm.
Gotteson, just where the hell did you come from?
I couldn't come from anything normal and good. No.
Because if I came from anything normal and good I wouldn't be
the Maniac I am. But since if everything in the world comes
from the world and is normal and good, I must be somehow
normal and good . . . somehow or other. Lying beside that girl,
the one I don't like to think about, all these spasms passed
through my brain, and I saw Bobbie Gotteson at each step of his
life . . . like on a stairway with real steps . . . Bobbie at the age
of nine, Bobbie at the age of twelve, and on and on and on to
where it almost drove me mad, *Bobbie my own age, Bobbie as*
myself! Can you imagine what that would be like—to see how
Bobbie Gotteson is your own age, the shape of your own body,
his face the same face as yours, all of it squeezed into you and
pulsing with life? Oh sweet Jesus, I would almost rather be back
on that bench with my pants wet and people sniffing and

giggling at me, I'd almost rather be back in Boys' Detention in New Jersey where some black kids dragged me into a stairwell and spread-eagled me and buggered me on our way out of the dining hall. I'd almost rather be gaping up into Melva's ugly sobbing face and hearing those words she spat at me, when she had to admit to herself that her Spider Monkey had gone the way of her other lovers, *just another puny floppy impotent white man!* she had screamed. That sinking feeling, that feeling of black swirling sick horror, the floorboards fading, the earth opening up to you, the way I felt when I heard what turned out to be the second stewardess out there on the porch fitting her key to the lock, oh Jesus, now for some inspiration! . . . and having to crawl to the door because I was so weakened by all the blood around me, even though it wasn't mine, and having to snatch at her ankles and yank her into the room, before she ran away, that incredible inexplicable feeling, that no song I could ever compose would get rid of. *Because there are some things that go beyond music!*

So, no. I couldn't come from anything normal, but everything is normal so I came from it and am normal. Unless I didn't come from anything and am not really here, though I seem to be sitting in an ordinary cell (not a padded cell since I am sedated) and I seem to consume the three-meals-a-day plus ten o'clock snack, and after my death professors at the Medical Institute adjacent to the prison will certainly do an autopsy on me. . . . I am going to leave my brain to the Neuropsychiatric Department of the Medical Institute, and my kidneys and liver and heart and eye corneas to the transplant-experts there . . . and my life-story to Antioch Paperbacks* and Vanbrugh Studios, free of royalties or fees, I don't give a damn any longer.

But where did you come from, Bobbie, and who are you?

Hate hate hate hate hate hate hate hate pity.
Pity pity pity pity pity pity pity pity hate.

---

*Despite his often uncanny powers of prediction, Gotteson was mistaken here. Homonovus Paperbacks and not Antioch will handle the unexpurgated *Confession*. Fritzie Del Blanc will play the lead in the film, produced and directed by Vladimir Jastsky, for Mega World Studios. The film is scheduled for release December 26 at major movie houses across the continent.

The girl with the fluffy red bangs—I know I'm skipping one of them, but that session was almost all blacked-out—made me hate her at once, the way she pursed her lips and crossed her slender ankles . . . the hate swelled into larger and larger balloons of hate, I could hardly hold myself back from her even before we were alone, and I knew how I had to rescue her out of that sluttish outfit of hers, I began to pity her so, the two of us wept together when we saw how hopeless it was. Then she somehow freaked out on me, maybe a long-delayed reaction to some bright peppy pills she had taken before I strolled by, and she giggled and laughed and began to rock in silent spasms of laughter, *as if she'd done all this before* and couldn't take it seriously. She pushed past me and ran into her closet-sized bathroom and tried to get the door shut, but I shouldered it open, and she leaned against the sink and pressed her damp forehead against the mirror of the medicine cabinet, laughing helplessly, hiccuping with laughter. I shook her by the arm, I grabbed hold of her shoulders to shake her sober. *Stop that! Stop that!* But it was like one other time a girl had freaked out on me and almost ripped my left ear off with her baby teeth, nothing can bring them down, nothing except time, and Bobbie hadn't time to wait for her. So I didn't wait. *What—what are you?—what are you doing?* she giggled when I began but still she could not be serious, not even my pity could make her serious, not even dying made her serious, it was all screaming helpless laughter the way a fat woman shrieks when someone is tickling her though this girl was skinny and—

Then I ran out of the building. Down the front stairs though there was also a back stairway. Right out front. Running, slipping, gasping for breath, not caring who might see me, anything to get away from her screams of laughter. *They can't even die seriousl!* I remember how Danny Minx was always joking. I remember all the jokes and clowning around at El Portal, even when I asked them to quiet down so they could hear my serious ballads, but no, no, they wanted so desperately to laugh, the mechanism got going and couldn't stop until they passed out. My mother, my original mother, did not laugh at anything. I know this. When she had me they sewed her up with coarse cheap black thread and there is nothing funny about that. I learned how to clown around and entertain, yes, but I never laughed much at my own jokes, and I could see how Mr. Vanbrugh was a serious man—he alone of the audience didn't guffaw when I fell backward and nearly broke my spinal cord—he was a gentleman—in a sedation-heavy sleep each night I dream of him arriving at my trial and stepping forward to be a character witness—though they said he had never appeared in a courtroom in his life, had never been served with a subpoena and never would be— *What are you? What are you doing?*—are not questions Mr. Vanbrugh would ever ask.

> as the tiny fish float in the harbor
> belly-up and harmless
> so parts of our brains float
> in parts of others' brains
> and no one is to blame
> for that single immense triumph
> in which we all float
> belly-up
> and harmless

ESCAPE IN BROAD DAYLIGHT
Passersby Do Nothing
To Halt Fleeing Killer

THE CURE FOR STAMMERING

—and for any other obsession—

MANIAC STRIKES AGAIN
And Again

—and again, though never with that daring reckless front-door busy-avenue escape, all of my disciples running and panting alongside me, bumping into me, Gotteson-as-a-boy colliding with a very surprised and angry black woman, last year's Gotteson (in his three-inch elevated shoes and the embroidered snug-fitting shirt from Tangier someone gave him) out of breath after the first frantic minute or two, his hand pressed against his side, whimpering with terror. But I,

Gotteson-who-is-now, kept my wits about me and ran through
an alley, climbed over a fence, jumped down, and ran down
another alley like a fleeing suspect in a movie or in one of the
Sunset Boulevard advertisements for a movie up there in
gigantic color—the fleeing suspect with his back to you and a
gunsight fixed on his head, through a telescopic lens. No
telescopic gunsight was aimed at me. *Passersby Do Nothing To
Halt Fleeing Killer*, the newspapers said angrily.

WITNESSES DISAGREE
Killer's Description Uncertain

I ended up in Hermosa Beach. I had some money: there
was a woman's billfold in my back pocket. I went to a
TacoBurger place and sat alone in a booth and began to focus
on the print in front of my eyes, someone's discarded *Los
Angeles Times*, and I tried to get the print to stop shimmering,
but for a while had no luck. I ordered a double TacoBurger with
chips on the side and a Coke, but had no appetite for any of it,
and asked the little-girl waitress if they had any chocolate bars
for sale, but she said no, she looked surprised and said no. She
watched me from behind the counter, standing there with
something held up against her chest—it must have been a big
menu—and the two of us were alone in the restaurant for a long
time, maybe twenty minutes, and once in a while I would
glance over at her and there she stood!—eye-to-eye in contact, a
smokey-faced sixteen-year-old, maybe a mulatto, and I never
touch anything except white people, a taste I share with Danny
Minx. She had thick wine-colored lips. She stared at me
recognizing me and the air between us was pulsating with short
sharp cries I could not interpret, and when I looked at the
newspaper the print danced around to taunt me—*illiterate* I
overheard someone say of me once, but that is a lie. I am not
illiterate. I can read fairly well, if I am not being observed or
crowded or jeered at. In the TacoBurger I seemed to be reading
about a maniac-on-the-loose, the words jumped around,
shivered, shimmered, then leapt into focus and were about an
unknown young man in his late teens, thought by some
witnesses to be black, by others to be Mexican, or Spanish, or
Italian, or something familiar to the area but not familiarly-

84

named, so there was disagreement and police were "baffled." One man swore to police that the "young man" was not a man at all but a husky young girl, dressed as a man. *She ran like a girl*, he claimed.

Except for my dizzy eyes I could take this without involvement. But my eyesight was failing. The girl came over to me silently and I felt her standing there, a little behind me, behind the booth I was sitting in. She asked me something. I couldn't make myself turn around. ". . . wrong?" she whispered.

20

The Redemption

Of the Maniac Gotteson

She was a long time dying.

No daring climb up the side of a building, no Spider Monkey illuminated by moonlight and cameras . . . not even any disciples, who leapt out of my head but grew dizzy and faded and failed and sank away as if into the floorboards of this shanty. I wrapped the cocoon around us. There were only two of us.

Jump-shots, athletic tricks of the camera, montage-freezings, no, nothing, only a cocoon for the two of us, for even my machete was lost—dropped on the stairway of that other building—and I had to use only a pair of scissors snatched up by chance, when the two of us knew all was lost. Except for the film or films the Prosecution will acquire and show in the courtroom, everything else is lost to the public, and the other films are on the black market, delivered by messenger hand-to-hand, and Bobbie Gotteson circulates underground without royalties or credit or public acclaim until someone, some night, shrieks with disgust and burns the expensive film while everyone else protests, *that collector's item!* and then all will be truly lost. Because I came to think, I came somehow to know, that the screen-test Vlad J. gave me at The Studio in Hollywood was not a real test at all, there was no film, only a trick to quiet Bobbie down. Bobbie needed quieting down, then. Bobbie needed a fake film-test so that everyone could get out of town.*

She put up no fight. It was a sigh, an unsurprised clutching, a broken-off scream. I came at her while her back was turned.

*For the record, Vanbrugh Studios deny both a real and a fake screen-test.

86

No screaming, no giggling. She wore a white slip. I thought of brides'-white in the movies, the costumes of girls seized and held aloft by Frankenstein or large apes and sometimes raised in the jaws of scaly monsters, a melodic screaming but no serious struggle.

I bundled her off to bed. I was not angry. I did not hate her. She was a long time dying and I did not know what to do, I had dropped the scissors and didn't want to crawl around to find them again, I was very tired, the signals coming to me were faint, fading away. Nobody shouted in this room. It was a back room in a shanty. My heartbeat slowed down. Sweat began to dry on me, all over me, so that I could feel it like a crust—slowly drying. I had never noticed that before. I carried her to the bed and lay her down and decided to lie beside her, just for a while, to get calm again.

Was there space between you two, Bobbie?

I gave her the one pillow on the bed and lay with my own head flat, I lay there not thinking or wondering, just the sweat drying on me, and if there was any pain to it, to all that bleeding, I did not feel it through her, she lay on her back and made only a whimpering sound, an *oh . . . oh . . . oh. . . .* My heartbeat slowed down. It slowed along with hers. My pulse subsided along with hers. Except for the blood there was nothing that had to do with a body. I lay flat beside her and turned my head to stare at her, quieted-down but afraid, and I asked her did she feel any pain . . . ? But she didn't answer. "Do you feel any pain?" I asked. "What is it like?" I asked.

She was older than sixteen. It said later that she was twenty-four. She was small-boned, smaller than Bobbie. Dusky-skinned. Dark-haired. Her eyes were half-closed but I could see that they were dark, probably dark brown, like my own. "What's your name?" I whispered. She did not answer. I could hear her breathing—quick short gasps—but both of us were slowing down, slowing, the signals that kept us in touch were fading. I raised myself on one trembling elbow to watch her. Her eyelids, her nostrils . . . her parted lips . . . and between us the soaking dark inkblot of her blood or maybe it was my blood, all my anger seeping out of me, fading, soaking into the mattress, pulsing out slowly heartbeat after heartbeat, helpless, coming to an end one ordinary weekday night, nobody watching, nobody filming, everything coming to an end. Lost.

I tried to stay angry with her. But. But it faded. I couldn't remember why I was here. I hated someone, but who . . . ? I didn't hate anyone. I hated them and then I pitied them, but now I couldn't remember what that was—*hate*—or what that other thing was—*pity*. I began to be afraid. I said, "Why are we here . . . ? What happened? What . . . what happened to us?" She seemed to hear me, she looked toward me. I saw her eyes shifting behind those dark lids. . . . She groaned. She tried to speak. I said eagerly, "What, what did you say . . . ?" but I did not dare touch her, I didn't want to hurt her. "Honey, I don't know your name! I don't even know your name!" I said. I could feel a heartbeat throbbing between us but it was not very loud. Oh sweet Jesus, what is happening . . . ? What is happening to us . . . ? I asked her what did it feel like, what was she feeling . . . ? I asked her what was happening. Her eyelids fluttered. I could see her nostrils widening. She said something, I didn't know if it was meant for me, I began to panic that she would die before she could explain, and I cried so loud that it must have frightened her, "Don't! Don't leave me! Wait! Wait —stop—wait—" But I could feel her going away. I could feel the heartbeat fading. If I had not been so afraid of her I would have grabbed her head to hold those eyelids open, I would have held them open with my thumbs, *held them open*, but I couldn't touch her, I stared at her and began to cry, I said, What, what is it like, what is it . . . ? What are you seeing . . . ? Who is there, is anyone there with you, wait, oh God please wait, don't leave me . . . don't leave me. . . . "Don't die yet, wait, don't die," I screamed, I begged, I got up from the bed and hung over it, wringing my hands like someone in a movie, even the smell of blood and the wet soaked bedding did not disgust me, I begged her to look at me, to tell me her name, to explain all this. . . .

"Why did you let me come back here with you, why did you bring me here, if you're going to die? If you're going to bleed to death?" I shouted. But she jerked her head on the pillow, her hands moved by themselves, no fighting, no clawing at me, she whispered something I could not hear but I was terrified to get close to her. "Wait—stop—what are you seeing? What's there? Where are you going?" I said.

"I. . . ."

I leaned over her. She said, "I . . . I . . . I can . . ."

"What?"

"I can see into it. . . ."

"What? What? What? What? Wait—"

But she did not answer. I stood hunched over her, staring at that face. It was moving away from me . . . I could see it changing. No good, I could only whisper to it, to her, I begged her not to leave me but in a whisper, and she was gone, she stepped over into what she had been looking at and went into it and disappeared and I, I was standing there in a panic, Gotteson standing alone sweaty and trapped in his body, sobbing long ugly melodramatic Melva-hoarse sobs because he is Gotteson the Spider Monkey and nobody else is Gotteson and Gotteson cannot get born into being anyone else, Gotteson is Gotteson is Gotteson forever. In this cell, in Court, in a gas chamber, in a morgue, out along the beach, rinsing his mouth with water from a rusty faucet or strumming his old guitar, Gotteson awake, Gotteson asleep, Gotteson in his essence or Gotteson surprised in an uncharacteristic mood, Gotteson Inside, Gotteson Outside, Gotteson clambering up the wall or toppling back down, jeered at or applauded, bouncing high with green capsules or dragged low by the forces of natural gravity, all's one Gotteson Gotteson Gotteson unrepeatable. There you are.

I began to scream. I screamed at her. "Why?"

I ran out into the street. Palm trees along the sidewalks, ragged and spidery, a city-smell to the evening air, and I ran out stumbling and shouting "Where is it?—the ambulance? Why is it so slow? Why didn't anyone call the police? Where are you all?" I ran out into the street. A car passing at about 10 mph almost ran over my foot and I pounded on the hood, and the driver gaped at me surprised while I screamed at him, "Get the ambulance! Where are you all hiding! It isn't too late, help me! Bastards! Bastards! Where are you all hiding—?"

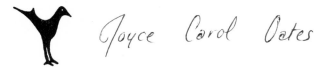

Joyce Carol Oates

Printed November 1976 in Santa Barbara & Ann Arbor
for the Black Sparrow Press by Mackintosh and Young
& Edwards Brothers Inc. Design by Barbara Martin.
This edition is published in paper wrappers;
there are 1000 hardcover copies; & 350 copies
handbound in boards by Earle Gray numbered
& signed by the author.

_54_

Photo: Graeme Gibson

Joyce Carol Oates has been called "the best young novelist in the United States today." *The Triumph of the Spider Monkey* is the fifth book by Ms. Oates to be published by Black Sparrow Press, the others being *The Hostile Sun: The Poetry of D. H. Lawrence* (1973), *The Hungry Ghosts* (1974), *Miracle Play* (1974), and *The Seduction & Other Stories* (1975).

Joyce Carol Oates is married to Raymond Smith, and both are Professors of English at the University of Windsor, Ontario, where they teach and edit the literary magazine *The Ontario Review*.